Table of Contents

Jazz Town

A New Orleans Murder

1

Michael K. Piper

© Copyright 2023 - All rights reserved.

Chapter 1

I wake up sweating. The blinds are open—I can feel the early morning sun boring into me, even with my eyes closed. My skin feels sticky, gloms of perspiration running down my cheeks—it stings. I wince, cupping my face; the palms of my hands detecting a texture to my skin I don't recognize—rough, jagged, punctured. I flit my eyes open, continuing to rub my torn-up cheeks. I check my hand to see if any blood's transferred. Clean. *Torn up cheeks?* This doesn't make sense. But my mind is groggy. Hazy. I seem to be operating on a 10 second delay. And then the headache starts—at first it's a dull drone, whispering its menacing cry into my subconscious. Then the pain kicks in, like a hammer beating me into submission. I feel as though my skull is breaking into a million tiny shards. The shards pierce my skin, leaving me battered and brainless in my bed.

My bed. I roll over, attempting to evade the brightness and heat infiltrating the room. But the mattress beside me is strange—wrong. I feel my way along the ancient fabric, the pads of my fingers dipping into something wet. *What happened last night? Did I piss myself?* Have I lost control over myself in such a short period of time? I'm momentarily ashamed—if only my parents could see me now; a drunkard resting in his own excretions.

But I open my eyes and suddenly, the guilt dissipates, replaced by the dread that drops from my pulsing migraine to my sour belly. *Blood.* I am surrounded by blood. No, no, no, no, no. *Mine?* The crimson liquid has infiltrated every layer of the bedding, from the blankets to the bare mattress. Maybe the headache is blood loss induced. Should I be checking for wounds? Wouldn't I be able to feel the liquid pouring out of me? Anxiety rises in my chest. My heart is battering against its cage. I jolt up, losing my balance as my feet collide with a sharp object. *Shit.* I've cut myself. More blood seeps out of my soiled socks. I'm crawling backward until I hit the wall, unaware of my own bodily movements. I just need to get far away from here. Get away from that evil sitting in my room with its tainted aura.

I run my callused fingers all over my body—I'm in my clothes from last night, but they've been removed of their pristine stitching and pressing. My white button-down is half open and stained. Dirt. Grime. Sweat. Bullet holes? Should I be looking for bullet holes? No. I would have felt that. I'm certain of it. How could I have been in such a dead sleep? I look as though I'm a corpse come back to life. I can't focus. I'm searching for injuries. Right. My torso is fine and so are my arms. My black slacks are frayed on the bottom, my socks riddled with holes and covered in mud. Where have I been? I don't remember this. Why can't I remember?

Should I be panicking *more*? My breathing intensifies as I consider my tepid reaction. Maybe I did something. Maybe I hurt someone. That would explain my appearance, my tattered room and clothes. I drank away the memory, forced it down and set it aflame with a bottle of whiskey. Or two. I'm not a drinker. At least I wasn't until I moved here. A cocktail is thrown in your hand everywhere you go—bartenders and showgirls beckon you into their buildings with a martini and a promise. The promise of a good time. The promise of a new life. The promise of something you won't forget. And yet I have—it's like my brain has been wiped clean.

I was with someone last night. A beautiful someone. Telula. Did I manage to get her back to my place? I've never done that before. I'm still a young man, barely in my 20th year. I know sometimes I lust for flesh but I want a woman I can respect and who respects me. I want a family. Fuck, will I ever have a family? I'm a murderer. I killed my future wife. That's what happened, right? I'm covered in somebody else's blood. It has to be hers.

Think, think, think, man. Something cut my foot. Focus. I scour the ground with my eyes—a knife. Jagged and bloodied. But that's my fluid on the blade. It's bright red. Fresh. The hole in my sock seeps more crimson. The knife is just beside the bed, strewn on the floor haphazardly. I think I heard it fall when I stumbled off the mattress. Or was it already on the ground? I should have been paying more attention. I've already made a mess of the scene. This is a crime scene. I need to see this from another perspective—an outsider stumbling upon the incident.

I try to remain calm as I evaluate the room. Panic won't help me, I have to concentrate. What happened here? The room is a disaster, which is saying something as it was never an immaculate space to begin with. I don't have cause for complaint, though, The Dog-House had put me up here on their dime—after performing at their club on a near nightly basis, they offered me a permanent position. I drew in a crowd, and right now, with the economy still struggling to reach anywhere near the same crescendo as the roaring '20s, they need all the help they can get to keep their business afloat.

The place isn't fancy by any means. The wallpaper is peeled and cracked—faded floral patterns marred by decades of water damage and rot. The bed is a double, but only one pillow was provided—the sheets are littered with cigarette burns, the stench of ash never lifting out of the fabric. There isn't a dresser or closet, merely a nightstand with two drawers and a chair in the corner. I hang my suits off the back of the chair to keep them as crisp as I can. I am grateful that I have anything to hang them on at all. A window etched into the right side wall exposes the bustling nightlife of New Orleans. Voices and music carry long into the evenings; the only silence falling over the city in the early morning hours. Crud has accumulated on the window panes, rendering it difficult to do more than lookout on a hazy scene and piece the imagery together in my mind more clearly. This doesn't always bother me—I like to stretch the capacity of my mind, to find beauty and romance in the everyday.

New Orleans is not what I imagined—growing up in rural Louisiana, I assumed anything bigger than my county had to be better. I kept track of all the great artists making waves on the radio; the names of the clubs they were performing in; the hotels they frequented. Everyone had lived in New Orleans at some point—whether they were discovered in a jazz club, or traveled there to garner the experience necessary to create their art—the biggest talents of our generation swarmed the area. My family believed I could be somebody—I worked my tail off to perfect the trumpet, my affinity for jazz and rhythm apparent even to those without an ear for melody. I aimed to follow in the footsteps of Duke Ellington and Louis Armstrong—their humble beginnings were evidence that I, too, could build a career for myself. I didn't have to be a shrimp farmer like my father.

But this magical place I had been hearing about through mumbles on the street and advertisements on the radio hasn't been the fairytale I had believed it would be. I don't mind working to make ends meet—I know that it'll always pay off in the end, but jobs around here exist solely in dank, underground kitchens. Clubs are seedy and rife with crime—between the gangsters, gambling, and hookers, any faction of a bar without a light on needs to be avoided. Hungry eyes defile me whenever I walk down the street—I know the locals can detect my otherness, my ignorance of their rules. I try my best to keep my head down and mind my own business, but the underbelly of New Orleans has a way of eating you alive.

I watched many a coworker overdose in the kitchens or get dragged out by intimidating men, muttering something about owing fees. I have heard horror stories about bright-eyed broads coming to town, only to disappear into a motel a week later and never be seen again. I have tried my best to avoid that same fate—I played at every jazz club I could, made nice with the owners, and promised nothing more than my music.

It hasn't only been turmoil—despite the unexpected decay of the economy and unmaintained buildings, I have still found moderate success. Though my tunes are not yet on the radio, the fact that I have a deal with The Dog-House means I am on the right path. Word of mouth has spread my name long and far, high and low. People no longer happen upon my music walking through New Orleans at night—they make a conscious effort to attend my shows. Fliers are passed around with my name showcased in black and white print—Mo

Millet. I had a friend of mine help me pick that out—the name. He said "Maurice" was too much for the tongue to tango; I was better off with something short and sweet.

"Maurice!"

Did somebody call my name? I snap out of it. I feel like the alcohol hasn't left my bloodstream. There's something wrong with me, with my behavior. I start and stop, start and stop. I should have run by now, right? But they know I'm here. My bosses are the ones who host me. My name and their establishment are attached to this crime—there's no way around it. Should I try to clean it up? That's what a guilty man does, though; he erases the evidence and goes about his day. *What time is it anyway*? The sun is still burning me, like high noon in the desert. But my groggy mind tells me it's early in the day.

I can't leave—not yet. I need to cover all my bases. I need to figure this puzzle out. I have to examine the bed. I try to stand up but my legs are shaky and weak. Is that pure adrenaline or is my body still going through detox? Maybe I'm ill from the stench. It infiltrated my nostrils, coated every fiber. I can't put a finger on it, but it's vaguely familiar. Putrid. Have I always lived a life surrounded by death? Was I fated to wind up a killer? The smell burns my eyes. I let out a cough from deep in my core—hacking and retching, I'm on my hands and knees. I feel as though I'm about to hurl. *Get it together, man. Fucking stand up*.

Slowly, the top of the bed comes into view. The violence is nauseating. I wish I could sit down again. I wish I could transport myself elsewhere. I wish I never came to New Orleans. Would things have been different back home? Would

I have avoided booze and dames and music and kept to my bedroom? I'm not a religious man, but I feel I am paying the same price as a sinner. Maybe the devil got ahold of me. I look at my spotless hands. How could this be? I am doused in horrors beyond my comprehension, but the only things that should be dirty are clean. Am I a strangler? Did I wash my hands before crawling into bed with a corpse?

There should be a body. I've strayed too far from it. The truth. There should be a body. A little more life in me now, I get closer to the mattress. A pool of blood and no body. That's odd. A gun, perfectly placed, glistening in that sickening sun, lies just underneath the pillow. That's not mine. I may have lost my mind but I know what weapons I own and that ain't mine.

I look around the room, as if I'll suddenly have an audience to send my disclaimer to. A jury. I'm a Black man in Louisiana, I'll never see a jury, much less be given a fair trial. I'll be sent to the slammer in a few hours, the rest of my life cut short. Over. How do I prove that's not my gun? That's not my knife, either. A gun and knife... something's wrong. I keel over. The acid in my stomach rages. I dry heave again. The bathrooms are in the hallway—shared stalls and toiletries. I feel like an animal sometimes, herded into my container for a bath, lacking the privacy a man has every right to. The staff would probably wash us if it meant speeding up the line. I try not to think about my dignity being stripped from me every day I spend in this city. I don't like to be down on my luck. There was a time I would have said "It could be worse," but as I stare at the mangled sheets before me, I know I'm at my lowest. At least I hope so.

Maybe the body's under the bed. The cot doesn't have much ground clearance, but it never ceases to amaze me what the human can accomplish under duress. I must have been stressed out in the midst of the act. That would explain the exhaustion; the bile building in my throat. I'm strung out, crashing from the high of taking another's life. How could I have done this? Telula. I loved that woman. Or, I thought I could love her. I was so excited to finally talk to her. To get close to her. Why would I suddenly have hate in my heart? Did she give me the weapons? Was I in such a drunken state that I fired the gun by accident? Yeah, this could've been an accident. I never thought myself foolish enough to do such a thing, but then again, do we ever really know ourselves?

I drop to my knees and I fear I may never get back up. I don't have the strength. Careening my back to drop my chin to the floor, I howl in pain. My muscles are sore. Tight. Like I haven't used them in years. I've aged 30 years overnight. I strain my eyes to peer into the darkness under the bed. Nothing. I throw a hand into the abyss, and come up empty. No body. There really isn't a body. So what did I do with it?

And then there's a knock at the door. My heart drops into my toes. My breath catches in my throat. Somebody's here. A maid? No, cleaning never gets done around here. It would be suspicious for this service to be offered today, of all days. Telula? Maybe she's come back. Maybe we agreed to go out for breakfast, have a date—a real one. But that would mean there was another woman in my bed and I killed her in cold blood. Or maybe it wasn't a woman. An intruder. Self defense.

Knock-knock-knock.

The knuckles on the wood are more insistent now. I swear dust is falling from the ceiling from the impact. Is it a gangster coming to collect a debt? Did the man I kill sell drugs for high-power criminals? Maybe he cornered me, attempting to pressure me into a purchase. Maybe he gave me a test run, and that's why I feel so alien this morning. So unlike myself. Out of my own body.

Knock... knock... knock...

I know what they're about to say before they even say it. "Police!" I get on my feet slowly. I don't want to make noise. I don't want the planks below me to bellow and moan under my weight. I can still run. Pretend I was never here. They don't have to find me covered in blood, surrounded by knives and guns. Because this isn't me. I am not a monster.

"Police! Open the door!"

I creep toward the window. My loafers are within reach. I slowly put them on, staring down at the street below, gauging my options. It's only a three-story drop. Every window has a ledge I can stand on. I'm getting out of here.

The knocking intensifies, bolstered by thuds as they ram their feet into the door. They're trying to break it down. I'm running out of time. Throwing open the window, I stick my head out. The cop car across the street is empty. There isn't a team of men after me. If I escape it'll take them a while to catch up. I throw a leg over the sill. The banging continues. I straddle the edge, bringing my torso under the glass and out into the fresh air. I see wood split as a policeman nearly breaks through. I have both feet on the window's ledge. I close the window behind me. And just in time, I crouch, allowing my hands to bear most of my weight as I begin to stretch my legs down to the next level, hoping to catch another ledge instead of tumbling to the concrete. I can't hear the commotion inside my room anymore. That's okay. I don't want to know what's happening. I don't want to know if they've spotted me.

The heels of my feet find the next ledge and I allow my grip to drop. I stumble for a second, my balance threatening to send me plummeting. But I stabilize. *Thank God*. I'm taking too long. I need to hurry up. I'm halfway down—jumping from this height won't kill me. I won't even break a leg. Do I risk it, though? I still feel achy, my limbs weirdly tense. I could sprain an ankle, and what good would that do me? I don't have a car. It's all on foot from here. Where am I even going to go? Should I seek shelter? Should I try to retrace my steps?

I close my eyes and brace myself for what I'm about to do—without giving it a second thought, I release myself from the ledge. The air feels refreshing on my grubby skin. A brief break from the horrors surrounding me. And then I hit the ground.

Chapter 2

I'm running faster than I ever thought possible. The fall didn't destroy me, or I'm too high-strung to feel any effects, at least. I bounced off the ground and sprinted out of sight—the streets are empty, so it must be morning. It's like a ghost town—the passions and activities of the previous night are mere phantoms in the yellow glow of daylight. The roads underneath my swollen feet are covered in pebbles and dirt. I can feel the spray of brown sand announcing my previous movements. I fear I'm leaving a trail behind me, a direct line to my current location. I should think of my next spot. Where do I go? Where do I begin?

Where was I last night? Let's start there. Telula. I keep coming back to her. Her voice—it rings in my ears. I was listening to it hours before I blacked out. She was on stage, her delicate, black hair tucked behind her ears. Her skin, like brown sugar, glistening under the stage lights. I can see her cheekbones when I close my eyes—precise, perfect, etched into her skin by a sculptor's hand. Goosebumps scatter along my forearms. The echo of her lulling melody makes me dizzy. What was she singing? I think I was too entranced to notice. I can't recall the words coming out of her mouth, only the shape of her lips, the honeyed texture of her voice.

Did she disappear? Maybe she did. Maybe she was stolen from my room. It's my fault for not knowing her. What's her last name? Where did she live? Who did she know? Why was she in New Orleans? I should have asked her these things. Perhaps I did—we were sitting in a booth, along with a man named Rene. How could I forget him? The stench, the cheesy attire... grime radiated off him like a cheap cologne. I know where to go.

The Pup Café is only a couple blocks from my hotel. The name of the establishment came to me like an epiphany, and now remnants of my affairs are collecting in the corners of my mind. Yes, Rene Bordelon. I think he owns The Pup, or at least, he made it seem that way. Maybe he'll be there. I can talk to him. Why did he introduce Telula and I? Did he? I force my brain to generate an image of that night, but I come up short. There's nothing clearly defined. Only fragments of a laugh, a drink, a secluded conversation. I remember feeling like royalty—alone with the most striking woman in New Orleans and her well-connected boss. Is that who he was to her?

The Pup Café appears before me—the green paint is chipping off the wood-paneled exterior. The lightbulbs that glow in the evening are shrouded in gray in the sunlight. The magic of the jazz scene doesn't permeate—it's only a memory that continues to be chased. A high that can't be repeated, but that one is always in search of. They know it's there. They know it exists. They'll always be attracted to its ephemeral nature. The walls are accented by purple trimming and posters lining the exterior—white paper decorated in red and blue lettering. The building is a rainbow—a treasure brought out by the rain.

Entering the building, the first thing that hits me is the dank air. The carpeting is alive with grime—it's fibers and bacteria and whiskey. Stains hidden in the darkness are fully visible in the sunlight filtering through the doors—large, blackened puddles riddle the red walkway. What I once believed to be a luxury is nothing more than a sham. A false hope. The walls are in better condition, but that's not much of an achievement—the chandeliers are cobwebbed, the picture frames smudged with thumbprints and dried food, but the paint job remains intact. Deep violet. Maybe the darkness of the color prevents any damage from showing.

The hallway feels long and unending. Perhaps my anxiety over what waits for me on the other side is exacerbating my journey. What if Rene is here? What do I ask him? I don't want to alert him to the possible death in my room, to the blood on my hands—I might not be able to trust him. What if he turns me in? What if he's already called the cops and they're on their way? I look down at my clothes—*fuck*, I forgot how mangled I am. There's no way I won't attract unwanted questions.

The jazz room at the end of the hall stares back at me with an emptiness that feels akin to a black hole. A void. I hate not knowing what I'm getting myself into. I hate not remembering what happened here. I can tell some of my lucidity has returned to me, but it's not enough to jog my memory. What if I never get it back? I'll be plagued by death forever, forced to reckon with a crime I may or may not have committed, never truly understanding myself and what I'm capable of. I don't like being out of control. I've always been a calm, even-tempered man. Or at least I've tried to be. I saw my daddy move through life with a good head on his shoulders, and a mild-mannered demeanor. He never stirred up trouble, never raised his voice, and certainly didn't step out of line. Maybe he wasn't an adventurous man, but then, we can't always afford to divulge in our fantasies. Perhaps my first mistake was dreaming of being a musician. I should have known—based on stories in books—that nothing good ever comes from pursuing greatness. The best we can hope for is survival. I wish my parents taught me that.

Maybe I came here out of greed—playing the trumpet is the facade I use to justify my lust for nobility. I felt I needed more than a quaint house and a doting wife—I needed danger, excitement, and enough riches to keep the children of my children out of work. I've never looked at myself this way before, but that doesn't mean I can't be blind to my true ambitions. Not anymore. There's no excuse for allowing my subconscious to operate my body. Now it's killing people—remotely controlling my arms, wrapping them around innocent victims. But I used a gun, didn't I? Or a knife? I still can't comprehend how it happened. Or why. That's what I'm here for.

The darkness of the jazz room expands and then takes shape. Circular tables fill the center of the room, all crowded around the half-moon stage. Largely hidden by massive red, velvet curtains, the platform looks measly without the spotlights. Another thing to be disillusioned by—the grandeur of performance. Have I been playing on stages just as meek? Do I have an inflated sense of achievement? I can't spiral right now. This isn't the place to lose myself in the commotion of my thoughts. All of the chairs are placed on the tables, the black and white checkered floors beneath them sloppily mopped. I guess there's no point in making the joint spotless when it's going to be ruined again tonight, and the next night, and the next. The cushy booths lining the back walls are undetectable in the dimly lit space—the room is windowless and too far removed from the front doors to catch any of the Sun's rays. Atop the bar are the only bulbs burning, and below them is the bartender, feigning business as he swipes at the same spot on the counter.

He doesn't look at me—maybe he's pretending not to notice. Maybe he genuinely never heard me come in. I guess my tread has been light—I'm on edge, afraid of setting off any alarms or raising any eyebrows. He's a stout man with a bald spot growing at the base of his head. A spindly mustache paints his upper lip, like he's been trying to grow one for years but could never admit he didn't have the right hair texture for such a look. Small, round specs sit perched on the bridge of his wide nose. I move in closer. He doesn't budge.

"Excuse me, sir," I say. My voice is hoarse—I'm not used to this cadence. Have I been screaming all night? Maybe I'm only a witness to the brutality that took place. I screamed, trying to stop it, but to no avail. Does everyone in my building turn a blind eye to violence? Gunshots and wailing, nobody thought to check in. Nobody thought to say something before it was too late. I'm getting up on my high horse, losing track of my mission. My stability.

He finally notices me, but it's marred by the disdain in his beady eyes. He's waiting for me to say something else. My opener wasn't enough. "Were you working last night?" He straightens, but remains quiet. His eyes narrow, which seems impossible considering their already faint size. "I ask because I don't recognize you," I add.

"Why should you?" he asks. His voice is brassy. His lips puckered.

"I'm a customer." I can't think of a better lie. Though, it's not really one. I must have slammed several drinks the way my head is feeling.

"So's everyone in New Orleans."

I want to laugh, but I stop myself. "I have... some questions." *Shit, I wish I was quicker on my toes.* I was never good at riffing.

"Yeah, you owe us."

"Huh?"

He pulls out a stack of slim pieces of paper and rifles through the pile. He hums, a sudden joy in his spirit. "Michael?" He holds up a slip with some scribbles in pencil I can't make out at a distance.

"Uh, no."

He scoffs. "Yes, I'm sure you're Michael."

"I'm Mo, actually. But you won't have anything there for me, I can assure you."

"Everybody's always tryna get a discount," he mutters.

I get closer, not wanting to ripple the tension in the air, but I need to see what's on the paper. "I wasn't drinking alone last night."

"So, if you're not Michael then you must *know* a Michael," he states matter-of-factly.

"I was actually here with Rene Bordelon and Telula..." I realize I don't know her last name. He notes the hesitation and pounces.

"Jeez, all you hooligans claim you know Telula. Can't even tell me a thing about her, I bet. You see a pretty girl in with the boss and suddenly you'll have what she's having. That's not how this works. Pay up." He's agitated now. I fucked up but I don't know well enough to retrace my steps. Hell, I can't retrace the steps of a murder.

"Well, I was getting to know her. Truly. Rene brought me to meet her—"

"And what does Rene got to do with you?"

"I mean... I don't know, really. That's why I came here. I have questions."

"About your open tab, yes. You need to settle."

"I don't think you understand, I didn't run a tab last night. In fact, I don't remember what happened. I just know Rene and Telula gave me something, brought me home, whatever. But they were here with me so they must know." I don't know why I'm telling him this. I'm giving him ammo. But I've lost my patience—how can I make him understand what's at stake when I hardly know it myself?

"You admit that you were wasted."

"I—yes. I guess," I stutter, flustered now. My armpits dampen as he grills me. Man, I wish I could shower. Maybe if I looked like a proper man, like myself, he would listen to me. I usually don't have a problem being heard. I know how to assert myself. I just can't find my footing right now. I feel like I'm already on trial and he's my unrelenting cross examiner. The jury of chairs and empty glasses watch the scene unfold without a hint of sympathy in their blank stares. I'm being a baby. Men don't whine.

"And you want to tell *me* what's what?"

"No, sir. I'm trying to explain to you—"

"Explain to me what? How to do my job? Who I work for?" He keeps cutting me off. If he would just listen to me, we could wrap up this tired conversation. He's trapped here with his boredom and sucking me into now, too. Picking an unnecessary fight just to have something to do.

"I need to speak with someone else."

"There's nobody else here, asshole. Or would you like me to call the cops?"

I'm taken aback. I can feel my hot cheeks turn suddenly pale. Cold. Riddled with illness. "You can't do that... over a tab?"

"You and all these fucking assertions!"

Why's he being so hostile? Can't I get a moment of peace? No wonder I have no recollection of the previous night, I haven't been given the room to breathe. To be at ease. A clear mind cannot be born in chaos.

"Listen, I'm not trying to cause trouble," I say, a quiver in my throat, "I just need to know where Rene is."

"What are you gonna do? Tattle on me to my boss? You think he won't side with greenbacks?"

"This isn't about money."

"Well for me, and for this business, it is."

"So why don't you check your receipts for 'Mo,' then? I don't care who you are, I'm not paying a random bill." I don't know where that came from. I've lost sight of my purpose. Of my composure. But I can't stop myself. I can't form the words in my brain before they escape my tongue. I return to that nagging fear—maybe this is who I really am. Hot-headed, ill-mannered, killer.

"Don't get smart with me. You're just a lowly souse."

"I'm a musician, actually. A paid musician. I don't think your *boss* would like to find out that this is how you treat your talent."

"I don't know you. He doesn't know you. You're a lunatic in garbage clothing. Probably homeless. Fucking grifters, man."

"This doesn't... this doesn't represent me." But it's too late. He's made up his mind. I'm just a bum trying to haggle. I can't hide behind my appearance. I can't propose that I'm a gentleman. I'm scratched up and dirty.

"Pay. Up." He's done talking to me. This isn't a discussion or a debate. I'm to do as he demands.

Even if I was inclined to bite the bullet, I don't have a penny to my name. Everything I own is tied up in my career—The Dog-House pays me in rent, there's nothing extra to pocket. All my earnings from previous shows went into my wardrobe and trumpet, keeping it crisp to the ear. I had to invest in my instrument, otherwise, why am I here? I've been scraping by, and happy to do so. All good things are worth the sacrifice. Or so I thought. Wasn't there supposed to be something better waiting on the other side of my hardships? I'm not one to demand a reward, but I really thought this time I deserved one. Foolish, foolish boy.

"I'm not Michael."

"Yes, you are. I'm not playing games, boy. Give me my clams!"

"What did Michael do last night?" Maybe I did give that name. Maybe he did see me and is just confused about the exact details. Maybe I was with another man and simply forgot. I can't pretend to have the answers.

"He did what all you bastards do. Ordered too many drinks, hit on every woman in the bar, put all his failures on a tab, and left."

"He didn't get up to no good?"

"He was rowdy, that's for sure."

"But he didn't start any fights? Leave with anyone?"

"How should I know? I'm a bartender, not a school principal."

"So, that's all Michael did? Drank a lot?" I'm deflated. This isn't anything to work with—generic intel, vague terms, common behavior. There's no way to know for sure this is about me. He could be lying through his teeth to make a buck. I'm not about to be swindled—I don't have the capacity to lose more than I already have.

"Pay up or get the fuck outta my bar," he says.

I resign—this was a whistling dixie. I'll be back on the streets with not a shred of clarity. A stray cat meandering down the back alleys. I want to spit on the floor, throw barstools against the wall, cuss out the bartender—he doesn't know what I'm going through. He doesn't know how scared and tired I am. If he were in my shoes, I'm sure he'd be just as resentful as I am for being treated like street trash. I turn to leave just as he asked, but this seems to aggravate him more.

"Where do you think you're going?" he hollers.

"You told me to leave. I'm leaving," I retort, and continue my exit.

He doesn't run around the bar to stop me. Doesn't do much of anything—just holds up the slip of paper and yells and yells. A bully without a backbone. "Get back here! You owe me! You'll never get in again if you don't settle! How's that for ruining your career!"

His voice fades as The Pup Café disintegrates behind me. On my own again, left to my own devices; left to scrounge up clues. Where am I supposed to go? The front doors appear like the gates of hell—I'm about to walk into the unknown. The abyss. An untimely fate. I wish I had a friend to turn to. A shoulder to cry on. And then it dawns on me—maybe I do have somewhere to hide.

Chapter 3

It's nearly noon now. People have started to emerge from their beds—storefronts are adorned with OPEN signs, shoppers mill about fruit stands and cafés. I wonder what day of the week it is? New Orleans doesn't align with any formal work week or schedule. There's no day of rest, no day of partying. Every night the streets live and breathe and every afternoon businesses operate. The only thing citizens seem to have agreed upon is the early morning—nobody opens their eyes until noon. It's wildly different from the countryside, where cattle and roosters wake you up before the Sun has even had a chance to break the horizon. My daddy left the house when it was dark and came back in that same darkness. I never saw him in the sunlight, but I could see his exposure to it in the deep lines of his face. His skin was dry and cracked—parched from hard work and intense heat. But he never complained—he had his woman and his children. All was right in the world.

The risen Sun means shadows have finally emerged between buildings. I try my best to appear casual as I beeline for the nearest patch of gray—I scan for cops but can't fully extend my neck without raising suspicion. People in this town mind their own business, it's just the way things are. Looking too hard at anyone or anything makes you a target. At least I know I won't be receiving stares for my heinous clothing. Everybody's used to this kind of activity—crime is something to be ignored, to forget about, to compartmentalize. We all know it's happening, but ain't nobody wants to get involved.

You never know who's operation you might be interfering with. Best just to keep your head down.

That's what I do—eyes on my shredded, leather loafers, making turns and sticking close to walls, my arms close to my sides. I become smaller, a mere speck in the crowds, in the hustle. I manage to safely transport myself to a rusty, green door behind a restaurant. I try the door handle, knowing it won't concede to my grasp—it's always worth a shot. Then I knock. Silence greets me on the receiving end. I can hear the echo of my raps infiltrate into the depths of the building. I knock vigorously—I know he's there—to no avail. I sigh, my shoulders drooping—does he know it's me? How can I address him without calling his name? And then it dawns on me; the intricacies of our morse code finding its way into my knuckles.

Ten seconds later and the door swings open. *Lenny*. I haven't seen his face in mere months, but it feels like years. He looks like he's aged, though I know that's not possible. Perhaps he's always looked this way and I never noticed, or the blue cast of the lights in the kitchen hid his imperfections. I can see the divots in his skin where acne used to dig its roots. I can see the yellow rims of his teeth. We're the same age, yet a decade separates our expressions. Lenny is my only friend in this town. Or he used to be.

He turns away without a word, but leaves the door open. A mixed message. He answered our shared password, but now he doesn't want to speak. People are strange—their convictions muddied, their behaviors enigmatic. I hate being on the receiving end of somebody's whims. Have I done something to spite Lenny? Have I not suffered enough? I'm one man... *Don't pity yourself right now. Just keep it pushing, Mo.*

Lenny walks into the kitchen, his large body filling up most of the doorway. From a distance, I can only make out the beginnings of rusted appliances scattered along the tiled walls. Red sauce paints his striped, loose pants. His apron is more brown than white. He attempts to keep his expression blank, but his down-turned eyes reveal his melancholy. I know he hates it in the kitchen—he's been working long before I got here and will be working here long after. I'm not sure what Lenny's goal is, and I bet he doesn't know either; I yearned to be a musician, while Lenny wanted a fantastic life. I never caught him humming a tune or reading a book. There was nary a day when he had a pencil or a paintbrush in his hand. He never spoke of fame or fortune, just the adventures he thought were waiting for him right outside the kitchen door. I don't see what he was saving up for or what he couldn't accomplish. But I haven't heard from him since I quit—I remember he ignored me on my final day, secretly seething that I dared to leave. I thought I rectified that, though. I invited him to watch me perform and he showed up. We had a couple rounds of whiskey and a laugh. I chalked up our waning communication to our busy schedules, assuming we'd catch up one day. I no longer think Lenny and I are on the same page.

I follow him into my old workplace, amazed that nothing has changed. Why would it? My sense of reality is warped—sauce doesn't jumble the brain this way. A blackout doesn't cause temporal amnesia. Something more sinister happened to me last night, I'm sure of it. And that's what I blurt out. "Something horrible happened."

Lenny sits on a stool, his bulbous belly staring at me like a second pair of eyes. He doesn't flinch. Why can't I get a reaction out of anybody? What will it take to make someone *care* about my situation? I just have to keep talking. I have to appeal to him. He can't be mad at me for quitting a shitty job.

"I woke up like this," I continue, gesturing to my ragged clothes, "and I don't know how. I can't remember anything crucial. I blacked out. I've never experienced that before, even when I've been real drunk. Which I don't like to do, anyway. Lose control like that. It wasn't me, you know? Somebody did this to me. I don't know what, and I don't know how, but my hotel room is covered in blood and I was left there for the police to find."

Nothing ruffles Lenny's feathers. I carry on, though. "All I know is I started my night at The Pup. It was probably one in the morning. I finished my set at The Dog-House and walked over. There's this girl there... a singer. Pretty. The prettiest damn woman I've ever seen. I've been going over there most nights just to catch a glimpse of her. Usually our performances overlap. But last night I watched her whole set, absolutely entranced, and the owner, Rene Bordelon, came over and invited me to her table."

A small sigh from Lenny. A sign of recognition? Remorse? "What?" I ask him eagerly.

"Keep going, man," he says.

"But that's where it stops. My memory, I mean. I have nothing left."

He gets up from the stool and saunters over to me. We stand side-by-side, our backs leaning against a table cluttered with dirty dishes and food scraps. The scent of nearly rotten food is almost comforting—working with Lenny wasn't bad. It was fun, even. I looked forward to seeing him every day, shooting the shit, making meals for each other on stolen food and time, behaving like we ran the place. We were rarely subjected to supervision, our boss too concerned with schmoozing the customers upstairs to set foot in the kitchen more than twice in an evening. I honestly don't know what the restaurant upstairs looks like, and I can hardly describe the food we prepared as authentic Creole. It seems to me we just threw together all the ingredients the boss could afford that week into various soups and salads and hoped for the best.

"Who was the woman?" he asks.

"Telula."

He purses his lips. "Look... I don't have much to say. But those names do ring a bell." He pauses.

"And?" I prod. I'm antsy. Desperate.

"Not much. I'm sorry, Mo."

I collapse into myself a little. "Remember when you gave me that name?"

"Yeah." He gives me a small smile. His edges aren't so sharp anymore. But he doesn't want to reminisce. "I heard Rene is a bad man. You could say the same about everyone in New Orleans, I know, but that's all I got. Telula's his girl. A prostitute, maybe. They've been consorting for some time now."

"She's not a prostitute..." I begin, but trail off. Can I really be sure of my judgments?

"I didn't say I was right. I'm just telling you what I know. The Pup is a place for criminals and Rene is the biggest one."

"What kind of crime?"

Lenny shrugs. "The usual stuff, probably. Drugs, girls, and gambling. Don't think there's much else a man can get up to."

"But not—"

"Murder?" He looks me up and down. "I guess that's possible. Everyone is capable of murder. Including you." He doesn't say it menacingly. He doesn't frame it like an accusation, just an uncomfortable truth.

"But I went dark, man. How could I do such a thing unconsciously?"

"Maybe you're just suppressing the memory. We tend to forget the parts of ourselves we don't like. Stow 'em away until they come up again. Use 'em and push 'em back down." I don't remember Lenny being so wise. I always viewed him as an oaf—a friendly giant, meandering through the maze of short buildings, always in awe of the unimpressive. I feel a pang of guilt for devaluing him. Nice people don't see themselves as better than others, do they? I've been wrong about myself. I keep coming back to this. There must be a sliver of truth there.

"Did I do something to you, Lenny?" I hit a button. I shouldn't have said that. Now he's walking back to his stool, anger infiltrating his disposition.

"I really don't wanna be involved in this." He's stern. It's a hard boundary.

"I need somewhere to go, man. I can't figure this out on the run."

"I don't want no gangsters or policemen knocking on my door looking for you. I'm not going to jail for your ass."

"That's not gonna happen. I promise."

"How can I trust you?" Another pointed glare at my disheveled appearance.

"It's not what it looks like."

"I don't know that, and neither do you. You said it yourself. You could be a whole looney."

"We're friends."

He almost laughs. "No we're not."

"Come on, man." The silence is awkward. The consequences of his declaration are harrowing. "What happened?"

My brain feels like it's been dunked in an ice bath. Lenny was my one point of refuge. I don't know anybody else. I don't have any other friends. He's setting me up for a lifetime of torture, and for what? What have I done to him? I want to be mad but I don't have a leg to stand on. My story is unbelievable, I know that, but I hoped he could at least entertain it for longer. Try to help me parse through the obscure details. The incongruencies. I would do that for him—that I'm sure of. I haven't lost myself that far down the rabbit hole to think myself capable of shunning a wounded friend. I know he wants to protect himself, but I'm not looking for a place to live or a witness for my testimony. I just need a safe space to lay my head down and think.

"Let me make you something to eat," he says. "You can stay here for an hour. But then you're gone." I know I should thank him but I don't—the acidic words burn the roof of my mouth.

I watch as Lenny cobbles together unrefrigerated ingredients—lettuce, onion, garlic, oil. He slathers the salad between two slices of stale bread and a couple hunks of chicken. I eat it furiously—it'll be the last food I get for a while. I didn't realize how hungry I was, but as I unhinge my jaw to take another bite, my stomach gurgles to life. Lenny watches me devour the food, his bulky arms folded across his chest. This is the first time I've performed for a hostile audience.

"I'm not trying to hurt you, Mo," he says after a while. "I just have to do what's best for me."

"Do you really think I did it?" I ask, feeling more morose than irate.

"It's not you. It's Rene and Telula," he confesses. "I don't like the sounds of 'em. I intend on staying far away from those people and that club. I said I wanted adventure in New Orleans, not the death penalty."

I pick at the remainder of my sandwich. How did I not know this about them? Lenny makes it sound like they're high profile outlaws. Did I accidentally get myself caught up in the underbelly of New Orleans?

"If you want my two cents," he continues, "you probably got drugged. That's the only thing I can think of that would knock you out like that. That is, if you're telling the truth."

"I am," I insist. At least, I want to believe what I say.

"And again, I can't tell you what kind of drug or from where. Rene probably has some crazy connections if he doesn't just straight up run a lab himself. That would be my theory. I don't want you to be a killer, Mo. But I got nothing else to offer you."

I let out a breath between my cracked lips that expels all the air from my body. My belly caves in. My ribs protrude. I have to make peace with what's happened. I have to accept Lenny's words. I don't have a friend or a dollar to my name—I realize that now. I can't act like a victim of it, either. I could have better prepared for rainy days. My daddy always told me to save more than spend, to put people before property, and I didn't really listen. I assumed everything would fall into place like it does for the main characters in fantasy books. Those stories were written in these same buildings, were they not? Should the magic not have transferred? It hasn't been that long since the city was in its glory days, and more of them might still be on the horizon.

"Don't hold out for Telula, either," Lenny adds. "I heard Rene's got plans for her and she's in on 'em. If you ain't kill her, he'll kill you for even looking at her. That's his *woman.*"

He's said it twice now, but the sentiment is going in one ear and falling out the other. He's at best her manager and at worst, a bit of a creep and a hustler. Sometimes you need to align yourself with whoever has the biggest pockets to make it in this world, even if they aren't the epitome of morality and virtue. I don't blame her for seeking stability—hell, that's what you could call my deal with The Dog-House. A way to make ends meet.

"I appreciate the advice, Len." And I mean it. At least my venture here wasn't as big of a bust as The Pup. I can half-heartedly point my finger at Rene. I can half-heartedly claim to be drugged. My turbulent emotions are likely the cause of a comedown, a fall from ecstasy. What the hell did that man give me?

"Stay safe out there," Lenny replies.

That's the last I hear from him—he goes about his business, loading up the sink with soapy water and getting out his cutting board to start prepping for the day. He doesn't watch me as I exit, and I don't call out a "goodbye." We go our separate ways a second time, and now I know it's final. I can't ever come back here and he's not going to come looking for me. At least

I got closure on one of the loose threads in my life before heading to the slammer. That's already more than most people get.

Chapter 4

The streets feel mean at this hour—the Sun has shifted again, but it's not yet setting. It's the middle of the afternoon, that awful period before nightfall where nobody knows what to do. It's too early to eat, too late to keep working, and always the hottest hours under the sun. I want to cover my face with my jacket for some shade, some relief, but these clothes should not be held up for all to see. God, I wish I brought my hat. I wish I had washed up at Lenny's. What was I thinking, leaving without even trying to get clean? Why didn't Lenny warn me?

Lenny. So peculiar how our relationship died. He behaves like a friend who's been abandoned, or an investor who's been strapped with my debt while I sign record deals for hundreds of dollars. We had different dreams—neither of us wanted to stay in that kitchen, but my ticket out wasn't going to be his. It's not like I could have vouched for him to The Dog-House, or promised him a solo. He didn't have an inclination for music—my reach would have been no use to him. I'm not even rich myself—I have nothing to offer and nothing to give. I simply moved my precarious predicament to a new location. Why should I feel bad about that?

Maybe we were never friends. Maybe my experiences are wrong. I could have misread our interactions, assumed he liked me beyond those kitchen walls. We were stuck together down there—he had no choice but to talk to me. Not doing so would have spelled misery for the both of us. Sometimes you make the best of a shitty situation, and that's all it is. I could have driven him away, too. Maybe I didn't ask enough questions, or show interest in his life. I don't know what his dreams are, after all, I only know the vague outline of them. He knows how I came to play the trumpet, how I craft a melody in my head on the spot. I lacked the curiosity crucial to nurturing a relationship.

Perhaps I didn't have any real friends back home, either. It's the same situation, is it not? Forced closeness due to limited space. Everybody tolerating each other because they don't have a choice. I'm a naive man to think the world is a friendly place. I took everybody at their finest, always assuming they approached me with kindness. I thought you got back what you put in, so I went through life with a smile and gung-ho attitude. I was excited about every person and every opportunity that came upon my lap. I was taught to be curious, to be generous, and to never let a bad day get you down. I'm like a child, still—innocently hoping for the best and ignoring the worst.

I can pin everything on that damn radio. That's how I wound up here. My father purchased a radio from a charity shop—we couldn't afford something brand new, and had to wait a couple years for the craze to die down before we could get our hands on one. We'd been hearing about the radio—this mythical force that brought voices and music into homes all across America. People could listen live while hosts announced new singles and local news. It fostered a greater sense of community, or at least that's what my mom said. She was always looking for ways to feel connected. Perhaps she was lonely in that house—without a job and without friends that belonged to her and her only, she needed something else to talk to.

We gathered around that radio most every night—gorgeous saxophones and perfectly harmonized trios filtered through the house. Everyone was happier when the music played—there was a levity in the air that couldn't be denied or mistaken. The radio is how I came to love jazz—it told me stories of talented men traversing throughout America's biggest cities to peddle their lyrics; it told me how to find pitch; how to arrange a series of notes. I learned how to play the trumpet by mimicking the radio's vast selection of songs—it took days before I heard the same song again, giving me plenty of time to practice. I liked the challenge, the reward, and my family fawned over my accomplishments.

A machine made me. It whispered details into my ears, laid out instructions for wonderment and financial gain. I was convinced by its sonic waves to give up my life in pursuit of frivolity. I thought the intimacy it became a conduit for in my home was an emblem of auspicious activity. But it drove me to New Orleans, with my silly suits and innocent mind. I have been tainted by the reality of city dwelling, of the world and all its inhabitants. People are cruel—it's an innate curse. What separates the cruel from the kind is only the matter of years it takes for one to wear their malice on their sleeve.

If someone doesn't have something to gain by looking out for you, they won't. Perhaps my community out in the sticks were nothing but leeches—my daddy worked on a shrimp boat, after all. Maybe he slipped them some fresh food on his way home. I'm a country simpleton who didn't understand the transactional nature of my being here—I am worth only what I provide. It's not Lenny's fault he can't help me; I am nothing but a step down the ladder. I have to be tougher, just like everyone else. My kindness makes me a target—they know I don't have the street smarts to navigate their deviousness. I won't see right through them.

That's how Rene got away with it. The owner of The Pup brought me to meet his number one girl. Telula had a voice that reminded me of my radio—it's like she was beckoning me home. I felt it radiate through my body, brand itself on my heart, on my soul. The radio ushered her to me. She was my calling. I desired becoming a duo—her voice, my trumpet. I had wild imaginations of touring together, driving fancy cars through back roads and getting on a different stage every night. We would write songs about our love, our children, our life. I had no cause to believe that my thoughts were fanciful. I had no reason to doubt my desires.

Rene knew how to fool me—he dangled treasure in front of my face. He didn't have to force me to obey. I may not have known much about him, but running your own jazz club is enough to be special in my books. Sure, his hair is greasy, the soiled strands poking out underneath his gaudy yellow fedora, and his Creole words are formed by a mouth spackled in gold, but that didn't have to make him a threatening person. Despite his unpleasant face, he is a slender man—nothing above average, and certainly not someone who can puff his chest out at anybody. If it came to a physical altercation, I don't doubt that we would be equally matched. His clothes are ill-fitting and flashy, as if to announce to his patrons that he has the clams, but not the class that usually comes with it. And he always has that damn cobra cane—he walks with it like it might give him prestige. It only highlights his smallness; he's dwarfed by his possessions.

Of course, Telula couldn't be in on his ploy. She's just like me—a dedicated worker, a slave to her craft. She'll do anything to aid her career, even if that means wining and dining some industry wannabes. What did she say to me? Did she say anything at all? Someone put a drink in my hand. I think it was Rene. It had to be. Telula wasn't a server—to have her passing around beverages would make Rene's entire operation look cheap. A poor imitation. She was bait, surely, but to what end?

Lenny said they were an item—a pimp and his girl, or two lovers. He never gave a definite version of the story. Maybe she rejected him too many times, crumbling her facade of vague intrigue and revealing her intention to use his connections for fame. For a way out of The Pup Café. Maybe somebody offered her a recording contract, or a residency at a different location, different town. Maybe she didn't ask to leave, she told him—her dissent made him furious. He loved her, doted on her, morphed her into a star, and she repaid him like this? He couldn't go on, knowing she was out in the world, thankful to be free of him. The thought corroded his brain, melted it into lava. He had to do something about it, but he didn't want to go down with her. He may have killed in the past and had the resources to deter law enforcement, but his links to her were too dense. Too obvious. If she went missing or turned up dead everybody would be looking at him. Soon his entire business would be under attack—if the police didn't give a shit, his customers would. The cops in this town leave their citizens to die, but sometimes the people are spirited enough to stick up for themselves. Or for those they deemed valuable. A beautiful singer at a popular club is valuable.

Along came me. He sussed me out, noting my frequent appearances at his club, but only to hear Telula sing. I didn't order women, I didn't throw a hand down in cards or place a bet—I got a drink and a seat, and stayed just as long as she did. Maybe he thought we were having an affair. Maybe I did her in just by following her around. How could I have been so stupid? I should have known that I was putting her in danger, that a woman like that would surely be taken by someone more powerful than me. It was juvenile to believe I would somehow woo her. Even if she wanted me, she couldn't have me. I created a new fissure in her life; something to fret over, something to miss.

I made myself an easy target—I would have done anything to be with Telula, and Rene knew that. I wonder if she tried to warn me. If only I could remember anything beyond sitting beside her, the lumpy seat beneath me ruining my posture, the glass in my hand making my palms wet. I felt awkward, embarrassed, like a teenager talking to his crush. I'm a handsome man, but before her I crumbled, became insecure. I ran my tongue along my teeth every now and then to make sure nothing was caught. I cleared my throat to prevent breakage. I adjusted the watch on my wrist, the length of my sleeves, the collar brushing against my neck. I remember all that but not what she said. Maybe I wasn't paying attention, too caught up in fluffing my appearance to really hear her.

Telula could have slipped something in my drink. My nervousness meant I was easily distracted. A flick of her hair and my concentration was elsewhere. She could have done it to protect me—Rene can't involve me in his schemes if I'm not conscious. Perhaps she had me taken back to my room, watched over me for a minute before leaving. She checked to see that the coast was clear, that I would be left alone in my drug-induced coma. She tried her best to save me. But Rene staked out the hotel, tracked her movements, followed her home, and snatched her right before she walked through the threshold. Dragged her back to my place and murdered her in my bed. In her struggle for life, she clawed at my face, desperately trying to wake me up. It all makes sense. This is the right answer.

I feel a rush of relief as the answers come to me. Finally, I'm free. I don't have to question anymore. It all makes sense. My dearest Telula, my heart aches for how you've gotten caught in the crosshairs. I'd like to think that she's still alive—there's still the issue of the missing body, afterall. How did Rene remove her from the building without being seen? Even in the dead of night people wander the halls. Nobody's on the same sleep schedule. Workers are coming home well into the morning hours and others are leaving for their first shift just after midnight. Doormen stand guard on a constant basis—the neighborhood surrounding the hotel is destitute financially, which means the people are desperate and hungry. They lurk around the perimeter, waiting for unsuspecting residents and tourists to walk by, their heads down, spatially unaware. Muggings and stabbings are a routine occurrence. With such high surveillance, how did Rene escape?

My momentary joy comes crashing down. *No, it doesn't make sense.* I wish I could revisit my room. The scene of the crime. I can't piece the mystery together without accounting for all the moving parts. I could be wrong about Telula. She could have been conspiring with Rene. I just can't see for what purpose, though. What does she have to gain by setting me up for a crime? I'm nothing to her, to either of them truthfully. Is it something I said in the moment? Did I make a remark about her body? Something vulgar? Did I get wasted and insult Rene's club? His business smarts? But the hit feels so calculated—surely they didn't decide to ruin my life in a split second, in a glance between lovers across the table?

I think I'm having a heat stroke. I forgot where I am—in the middle of the street, my loafers covered in dust, my forehead slick with sweat. People scurry around me—they don't want to garner my attention. I know they fear me. I know they think of me as a dastardly bum, waiting to snatch their purses or pull a knife on them and demand payment. I didn't think I could sink this low—I may be a poor man but I'm not a thief. I'm not a threat. I've always been able to get by without much and not feel the effects—I still have nice clothes, money for my hobbies, and a place to rest my head. Losing the social graces of my peers is a fate worse than poverty.

I need people. I need friends. I need family. I've had all three taken away from me before I even opened my eyes this morning. I'm alone in this city—nobody wants to take me into their home, hear my struggles, and try to help me out. I'll be alone in my jail cell, my family never hearing about my arrest. There won't be anybody to inform them—they'll spend years without word from me, and just assume that's how I wanted it to be. To abandon them without warning. To never be traceable again. My mother will mourn our relationship. My father will be quietly resentful. I'll navigate the legal system alone, probably land myself additional time in the slammer with whatever scum of the earth lawyer is appointed to me.

He'll take one look at my case and pronounce it a failure, collect his check and run. I'll wither away in my solitude, yearning to get back what was stolen from me. I will die with nothing. An anonymous grave will be dug for me.

I want to sit in the middle of the street. Give up. Everyone's afraid of me, anyway. I have nothing to lose. The police will come for me eventually—there's no point in trying to outrun them. What am I preserving myself for? A meaningless existence? I was silly enough to believe I could be a musician. I gave up everything to move here. I had my loved ones rally for my success. And I have come up empty handed. Jaded. Spoiled.

"Hey! You there!" I hear a booming voice cry. I freeze. My malaise suddenly dissipates. My deterioration halts. "Hands where I can see 'em!"

This is it. I have to decide—do I give into my despair? Do I let Rene steal my life? My freedom? Am I really ready to die? My fingers twitch, my arms ache. Surrendering might be the easiest way out. I've never liked easy, but I'm tired. I'm always tired. I gave it my best shot, didn't I? This is what the world gave me. It chewed me up and spat me back out.

"I'll shoot!"

No. I'm not ready to give up. Not yet.

Chapter 5

I take off down the road. I don't look behind me, I don't need to. I can feel their guns aimed at my back, the direction of their barrels boring into me like a beam. Every second I spend checking their whereabouts is a second wasted. I can't get distracted by the past. The crowds are thinning as I push forward—I need to retreat, to make a break for the town square. The afternoon gives way to the early evening, which means bars and clubs will be opening soon. The activity will draw groups, who'll meander in the streets between buildings, causing traffic jams and blocking views. It's the perfect place to get lost.

I got too caught up in my head. I did this to myself—roaming around in the open, my clothing in shambles, my face bloody and sinister. I keep forgetting I'm not back home, in the safety of my small town. I'm not dumb enough to think Black men aren't in danger everywhere they go, but I at least know what places to avoid, which corners to never be caught in. Some neighbors couldn't be trusted, and certain bars were guaranteed a phone call to the police. I could lead a sheltered lifestyle there—stick to the main roads, only interact with family and friends, and don't go out alone at night. It's confusing to be surrounded by so many people that look like me. You'd think it'd be better, that because we're the majority we'd have the benefit of our numbers. Nope. The White police force lines their pockets by throwing us in jail.

I wonder if they're after me intentionally—am I a suspect wanted for murder, or did I simply look like an easy target?

I guess I just assumed they pulled the records of who stayed in that room, contacted my boss at The Dog-House, alerted all the local policemen to my age, name, and appearance. In a just world, law enforcement would act that way to catch a threat to society. But this is New Orleans—the less black people on the street, the better. A dead club singer might not even bother them. Telula's not a priority—bringing her justice isn't on today's docket.

I'm farther out from the town square than I thought. How did I get here? Was I wandering or standing still? I don't recognize the buildings around me. They appear more residential than business-oriented. I probably wandered into the urban version of a hamlet. I have to figure out a way back. I can't turn around—I'll walk straight into detainment. Maybe this is a good enough ploy to shake them off—they'll never suspect my coming here. I only catch brief glances but I can tell the apartments here are nicer, upper-class. The air is free of garbage and bodily fluids—the wealthy must pay for their streets to be cleaned on a regular basis. I don't fit in here. I wouldn't believably have any place to hide or shelter here. Hopefully, this was an accidental success.

Then again, if anyone is going to call the police for a neighborhood disturbance, it would be the White people clutching their curtains and watching me roam the roads from the safety of their luxurious rooms. I bet that's why the police are following me now—a strange, probably drug-addled black man had the audacity to be in a public space. My parents would likely bust my chops for being in this position—I did it to myself. I allowed sketchy clubs to put me in seedy hotels. I hung out with the wrong crowd—kitchen hands and gangsters.

I believed everyone was benevolent and I assumed I was too innocent to be corrupted. I thought that, at worst, I would be left alone. I left the confines of comfortability and reliability for the unknown—this is the price I have to pay for it.

Eyes seem to be glaring at me from all directions. I have that awful, sinking feeling. I am not out of the trenches. I try to pick up my pace but a cramp is forming in my ribs. I didn't realize how exhausted I am. How dehydrated and hungry. My tongue feels heavy, like it's swollen and blocking the entrance to my throat. I try to swallow but there's nothing to go down. My mouth is a desert, my thirst unquenchable. My ankles hurt. Maybe my jump from the side of my hotel room wasn't as easy as I thought. I can hear my ligaments shifting and cracking as I sprint. I'm wheezing. Slowing down. I don't want to give up, but maybe I have to. I'm not strong enough for this.

I decelerate to a jog and hide in the shadows cast by a building. I take a moment to observe the area—monotonous, posh, and foreign. I still have no idea how to get where I want to go. I wish I could pull someone aside and ask them. Or knock on a door. Nobody would answer me even if they were here. They would watch me flail and beg and cry and use that as evidence for the police when they denounce my sanity. My lungs burn and ache. I feel like I'm in a steam room trying to inhale the scorched air. The rims of my nostrils tingle painfully.

I hear the unmistakable tread of footsteps in the distance. Running. Shouting. Fuck, they're still after me. What if I stop here? I could potentially hide. They may not even see me—they're probably looking straight ahead, their focus only on the path directly before them. They aren't anticipating my diversion. Or my stopping. It's not like they'll see me duck in here. There's a backyard not too far away. It's in my eyeline, not theirs. I can see wisps of green, gently swaying over the clear, blue sky. A garden and a breeze. An oasis in the midst of a war. I just need to go a little bit further and I'll be fine. It'll be the worst few minutes of my life, and then it'll be over. Just keep going. Break through to the other side. *Go*, man. *GO!*

I take off. I hope I didn't make the wrong choice. I hope I didn't leave myself exposed. It's not like there are many places or doorways to lodge myself in when I suspect they might be getting closer. That they might detect I'm down here. The crunch of the earth beneath me has silenced their approach—I know they're still encroaching, and my noise level is concerning. I've shrugged my own protective armor and have sought risk over guarantees. But it's okay. The garden is almost within reach—I can see a low, amber wooden fence. A porch surrounded by bushes and flowers. Wind chimes gently thumping against each other.

What nags at me the most is the feeling of regret—I hate thinking I made a mistake. I desire to take control of my life, to own up to all my decisions and missteps. If I land myself in prison for trying to flee to freedom, I need to bear that cross. If moving to New Orleans in pursuit of a jazz career is the life I sought for myself, then I can't be mad at the outcome. Disappointed, yes, but not angry. If I hadn't done it I would have spent my years waking up every morning with the same burning question: *Is there something more for me out there?* I could have done all the things I wanted to do—even now—such as get married and start a family, settle down somewhere in a modest home, but there would have always been a nagging sensation deep down; I should have at least given my dreams a shot. I'll never know what I would have regretted more—staying or leaving—but I can't torment myself over that. Not now. Not ever. I need to learn to stick to my guns. To make poor judgements and learn to cope with the fallout. Move on from it. Become bigger and better. It's the only way I'll get out of this mess, too. Or at least try. Make a decision and run with it. Problem solve. Uncover the mystery.

"He's over here!" a voice shouts.

So close. So fucking close. But my hideaway is under siege. It'll no longer be an adequate place to veil myself. I hop over the fence into the yard anyway—at least the obstacle will pose a potential problem for my pursuers. The length of the overgrown grass will provide some cover. These are small victories, albeit temporary, but they buy me precious seconds of time.

In the garden I decide to take a glimpse behind me. I can see the blue uniforms between the blades of grass. They're on my tail. How did they catch up so easily? I had lost them for a moment. Evaded them entirely, even. Now here they were, chasing me to my demise. *Keep going.* I trample herbs as I scurry, silently apologetic to the houseowner. I don't attempt to get their attention or beg for mercy—it's a bootless errand. I do, however, spot another backyard attached to this. I jump another fence, and plunge myself into a series of miniature jungles, all in pursuit of a place to rest. To conceal myself. I spot sheds and pools and unlocked doors, but the police are too close for this to make a difference. I need to lose them in something dense. Impenetrable.

Another fence. I try to leap over it without slowing down and end up getting caught. With one foot on the outside, I fall, face first, into fresh soil. My ankle yelps as I attempt to free myself. The policemen are still near, branches snapping underneath their stompers. I press my hands into the dirt for stability, but it's futile. The wet ground is slippery. I collapse. I shake my foot, the entire fence groaning, but can only feel the leather peeling off from the splinters. "Come on!" I squeal. The panic is overwhelming. Unbearable.

"Put your hands where I can see them!" Their cheaters break through the shrubbery.

One last effort. One last try. This is it. My foot wriggles out of the gate. I quickly get on my feet, my body sliding in the soil as I regain my balance. I'm almost out of luck. There are only so many backyards I can cut through, and many more hurdles to slow me down. To ensnare me. I feel as though I've been running for hours. The Sun looks like it's setting now—that's impossible, isn't it? I didn't know I had this endurance. I'd be more enthused if my life wasn't on the line.

And then a shop appears. Bounding over my last fence, I come across a corner store. I don't check to see if it's a change in location, a bustling shopping strip as opposed to a quiet neighborhood—I simply charge through. The windows are covered in old newspapers. The front door is slightly ajar. I don't catch the name.

Pulling open the door, bells jingle to announce my presence. *Can't I do anything without an alarm going off?* I don't see the shopkeeper behind the cashier's counter. A large register sits on the cherry-stained wood. The wall behind it is lined with stacks of cigarettes. I could use one right now—the head rush might provide some much needed clarity, or at least a little energy. The cops likely saw me come in here—I have yet to put any distance between myself and them—so I need to keep it pushing. Thankfully, the shop is tightly packed. Aisles are indistinguishable from each other, with various goods spilling all over the place. It's unclear what this store is meant to sell—groceries? Toiletries? Books? The eclectic wares are distracting.

I dip into the first aisle and head to the furthest wall. I step out of view, huddled behind an array of canned food. I hold my breath. Wait for the bells to announce the policemen. I bite my lip so it doesn't quiver. Move on to the next aisle. Wait. And then the bell tolls twice. My vultures have arrived.

"Excuse me!" One of them shouts. I'm not sure who he's addressing. But when there's no response, he slams his fists on the counter. "Excuse me!"

I want to move while they're occupied, but my loafers make noise on the tiled floors. Even lifting my toes lets out a tiny wail.

"Hello, sirs, what can I do ya for?" another man says. Must be the shopkeeper.

"A fella came through here. Cropped hair. Dark skin. Gnarly looking," the policeman describes.

"Uh…" the shopkeeper begins.

Please don't give me away, man. Please.

"I don't know what you mean."

"Fuck off. This place isn't big. You've seen 'im."

"I'm sorry, sirs, you're my first customers all day."

Their conversation masks my movements. I tiptoe along the back wall until I reach the door to the storage room. Opening it will be a struggle. The creak of the turning knob. The groan of the ancient metal scraping against rusted hinges. Is it worth it?

"Bullshit. Why are you protecting him?"

"Sirs... I really don't know what you're talking about. If he's in my store I didn't see or hear him. There's nothing else I can say. You're free to look around."

"Fucking colluders. You people are disgusting."

I pull the handle just as they finish talking. Halfway there. But now they're roaming the aisles. Looking for me. Sniffing me out like bloodhounds. Their stompers thud against the floor. They knock things over. Make snide remarks. They're blundering through the store, giving me all the noise I need to mask the door opening. I take a deep breath and pull it open.

Gritting my teeth, I lodge my foot into the opening, giving myself time to peer around the shop. They haven't acknowledged the sound. They haven't started running. So far so good. I worm through the crevice and suddenly find myself on the other side. The door gently closes behind me, my sweaty palm guiding it into place. Softly. Slowly. It's dark. Only the faint outline of a staircase glows in the darkness. I once again pause, straining my ears to detect any imminent danger. Nothing directly outside. I descend.

My footsteps echo like tap shoes on a freshly tiled floor. They're going to check the basement whether they hear me or not. It's only a matter of time. I make my way through the maze of undetectable objects, my hands in front of me. I'm feeling the air, anything, everything. I don't think my eyes are adjusting. What if there's no way out? Not every basement has a door or a window leading to the exterior. Should I find a place to crawl into and hide? Will the cops give up the chase after a quick sweep of the store? Will they assume I used it merely as a passageway and am already on the other side, or do they know

I've stopped here? Is this a good place to hole up? The store clerk obviously heard me come in. Though he didn't check on me, he does seem to be protecting me. Maybe I'm reading his behavior with too much kindness. After all, if Lenny wouldn't have my back, why would a stranger with nothing to gain?

I should look for a way out. I can't trust anybody—that much is true. The basement seems vast—I can no longer detect where I came from or which direction I'm heading. I'm lost in a hellish maze. Constantly tripping. Scrambling. I hope they can't hear me upstairs. My heart is thudding so violently in my ears I'm not sure I'd be able to detect the door opening. I have to calm down. Just enough to stop huffing and puffing. Just enough to ensure I don't give myself away.

And then there's light. Just a spotlight at first, illuminating the rows of shelves around me. As I move toward it, it engulfs the space. At least it feels like it does. It's my only scrap of hope. The beam takes shape as I get closer—an outline of a doorway. *Holy shit.* My outstretched hands meet the cool metal, first. They slide their way around the material, the pads of my fingers making a slight squall as they drift. I find the doorknob and pull. It won't budge. *Locked?* I twist and turn it. Pull again. Nothing. Another direction for the turn. Another tug. I'm locked in here. This can't be happening. I've come so far....

Feet on the steps. The unmistakable groaning of wood under human weight. They're here. They've finally come for me. I squint as I try to make the doorknob come into plain view. I feel like I'm conjuring false fantasies. I rub my thumb along the lock—the keyhole is large. I could probably pick it. I drop to my knees and scour the floor for anything thin to jam into the cleft. Voices become more apparent. They sound like they're bickering. With the shopkeeper? I can't tell how many people are down here with me. I discover something metallic on the floor. I pick it up, roll it between my fingers. Sharp, like a needle. *Perfect.* I jimmy it into the keyhole. I don't worry about the sounds. I need to get out. They'll discover me as soon as I open the door, anyway. Their conversation is louder now. Their words are almost clear. I wriggle the needle some more. I hear the click. That beautiful click. Without meandering, I turn the handle and swing open the door, bolting as the policemen realize what's happening.

"Get back here!"

But it's too late. For them, at least. I've come upon the town square. Finally, a lucky break. The area is just as busy as I anticipated. I easily worm my way into the crowd, discarding my jacket as I weasel through. It's the only thing I can change about my appearance. Hopefully they'll have a harder time identifying me from the back with one article of clothing missing.

The bustling epicenter is anxiety-inducing—I can't get my bearings. My sense of direction is lost in the hustle. I keep my head down, my stride in step with the others, and cross to the other side. In an alleyway, I quickly glance over my shoulder. I don't see any uniforms. I don't see any stares darting my way.

"Hey, you!" A shouted whisper beckons.

I flinch. *Fuck.* All that for nothing.

"Psst!"

Huh? That doesn't seem authoritative. I look around and notice a woman peeking her head out of a doorway. She waves at me, prompting me to come closer. I listen to her.

"Come inside, my boy," she says. She nervously glares behind me. "Come, come," she repeats. I'm taking my time. She obviously hates that. She's in a hurry. For what? I allow her to pull me by the collar and drag me inside the building. Curiosity may kill the cat, but it can't get much worse for me, anyway.

Chapter 6

The cuckoo clock on the wall ticks mercilessly. It fills in the gaps of our silence. Of my discomfort. I shift on my chair, the old wood announcing my restlessness. I don't know why I followed her up here. I don't know who she is. She hasn't told me a name. An age. If she's related to me. Her black hair is done up in a French twist, her chubby body compact in a pink dress. She looks like she's had a couple kids and the lines on her face corroborate this. Her brown skin is soft—I felt it when she brushed against my neck, grabbing my collar. She smells of vanilla and cookie batter. A flutey voice and a sweet face. She reminds me of my mother—the gentle nature, the perfect lipstick, the silently desperate eyes. I want her to be as kind as she looks.

She's in the kitchen making us tea, though there isn't much distinction between each of the rooms. The kitchen, living room, and dining area are all one, separated only by furniture. I'm used to walls springing up throughout a house, even when there isn't enough space to justify it. This layout is peculiar. I truly understand how far from home I am now. I can't even recognize the apartments or the décor. Even though I'm in the same state, nothing is familiar. Nothing is safe.

Her kitchen is wallpapered with white and yellow stripes. Berry colored carpeting covers most of the floors. And that damn cuckoo clock keeps ticking. The bird springs out on the hour to mock me. To jeer. I'm sitting at a small, square table covered by a table cloth that matches her dress. The kettle sings as it reaches temperature. The woman pulls out two chipped mugs from her cabinet.

When she sits across from me, she flashes a wide smile. The glee is ill fitting, considering how she found me. I'm still a disaster physically, and now I reek, too. The perspiration has accumulated on my clothes; on my skin. I look like the guilty criminal I just might be.

"I'm Angela," she says, picking up her cup to take a sip. I don't know how to respond. I don't think I should give her my name. You never know what someone's intentions are. Maybe there's a price on my head. "You're Mo, right?"

I bat my eyelashes furiously. Purse my lips. *What*? "How did you know that?" I ask. The thing I dreaded is true—I'm a wanted man with a warrant. My face is plastered on every building and street lamp. I'm an insect caught in a spider's web. My mistakes keep stacking up.

"Oh..." she half-laughs. Fidgets in her seat. Swats away the question with an embarrassed hand. "I watch you play at The Dog-House all the time."

That's not what I expected. I wait for her to explain herself. She waits for me to acknowledge her. Maybe she wants me to say the same—that I recognize her from the audience. She's my most appreciated, loyal fan. But I don't, so she blathers on. "I was so happy when they made you a regular. People think jazz is for everybody—they can just pick up an instrument and go. I've seen so many talentless men come and go through these clubs. It's sad, really, what passes for music these days. But you... you remind me of the greats." She pauses to shrug, suddenly sheepish.

"Thank you, ma'am," I say, trying to ease some of the tension.

"And I don't mean to flatter you," she corrects. "Well... not entirely. It's just that hardworking men rarely get the credit they deserve. Not until it's too late, that is." She nervously piles more sugar into her cup. "So, I don't want you to think unkindly of me, now. But I have a confession."

We share a gaze. I think I can anticipate what she'll say but she has me stumped. Mystified. "I followed you the other night. Many nights." She blushes. I don't budge. I keep my focus trained on her. Maybe that's why she's squirming—my stare is too intense. "I promise it wasn't to harm you," she continues. "Though I hope that's not what you assume. I just love your music so much... I wanted to see where you'd go next. I tried and I tried to work up the courage to talk to ya. I didn't want you to think I was some cockeyed old lady trying to get you to bed or move in with me. I just wanted a conversation, is all."

"So, you were following me to The Pup?"

"Yes." A moment of silence. She fills it. "I don't want you to think I'm a stalker. Oh, nothin' like that. I dunno where you live, who you know, where you come from. Nothin,' nothin.' But in my following you, I noticed something awful I think you should know about."

"Does it have to do with this?" I gesture to my tattered apparel.

"Maybe. How did you end up that way?"

I click my tongue. Should I divulge this to her? Would she believe me? If I tell her now, would that impact what information she gives me? What story she weaves? "I wanna hear what you have to say first, ma'am," I retort.

She nods—this is a fair bargain. "Well, I sat close to ya, I'll admit. My courage is weak—I needed a way to force myself. But last night, when I finally felt ready, I noticed a very bad man approach you. I know he's a big name in New Orleans, but... those who know, stay away from 'im."

"Know what?"

She shivers like a gust of cold air just tapped her spine—the ghost of Rene whispering into her nervous system. "I'm not sure that I can say. But by the looks of ya, you've already found out. And that girl... yeah, I saw 'im bring you to that girl. She's just as devilish as he is."

I sit back in my chair, deflated. This is the second poor testimonial of Telula. It might be high time I admit she's no good. Angela hasn't gone into many details, but I'm hard pressed to find a reason for lies.

"She's a pretty face, I know. Men always have a hard time with this, but it'll save you from more heartache in the future. She ain't nothin' more than a lackey with good cheekbones. Maybe even an instigator. Lord knows even Rene would listen to her."

"Did I leave with them?"

She pauses for a moment to think. "No... no..."

She's not confident in her assertions. She's hiding something, I can see it in her eyes—there's a ruse she doesn't want to expose. Perhaps she hasn't thought it all the way through. Perhaps she's older in age than I assumed and she really can't remember the details correctly. But something's off.

That's what my gut says. I have to start trusting my own instincts. I let her relay her story regardless.

"No, you left just after three. They stuck 'round, hung out at the bar. I caught what they was saying, too." She gets up for a second round of tea. She holds up her empty cup and points at the kettle. "Want another, sweetie?"

"No, thanks." I hate that she's stalling. She's probably trying to piece her story together on the fly.

"They was talking all sorts of evil. I heard conniving and plotting." She rustles through her drawers for another spoon to dirty when she mixes her milk and sugar.

"What did they say, exactly?" I attempt to coax her.

"Like I said, dear, I can't remember all the details. I just know it struck me to my core. My bones hurt at the sound of it all." She returns to the table, a slight hobble in her step. The glass cup and plate clink together—she has a shaky grip. "Now I see you... lookin' that way. I know they musta did something."

"How did you know, though? That I needed help? Are the police—"

"Aht. The police are always stalking through here. They don't bother me none."

"Yeah, but... you had to have known they're after me, or else you wouldn't have invited me in."

"You ain't in the papers if that's what you're asking."

"Alright..." I'm confused. She says she can't remember Telula and Rene's conversation and yet she knew to keep an eye out for me. Knew I'd be coming this way. Something's not clicking into place.

"I told you—they got a plan. A nasty one. I didn't expect you to show up at my door, but I was anticipating pulling you aside tonight at The Dog-House, letting you know what's up. Guess they got to you before I could."

I take a sip of my tea. Watery. Vaguely herbal. Cheap. I can't grimace, though, that's impolite, and this is the only source of water that's touched my lips today. "I gotta be honest... I woke up with no recollection of the night before. I know 'bout as much as you're telling me—that I spoke with Telula and Rene. I also can't remember how that conversation went. But a murder's taken place."

"How do you know that?"

"Well... nothing for sure. Just a whole bunch of blood in my bed. On me. I don't know whose. I was alone in my room. Nothing but me and this mess. But cops have been chasing me all day. I don't know what they want and I'm too afraid to ask. I ain't going to jail for this, ma'am. I can't."

"Hmph. That Rene... yeah, he's done somethin' unforgivable."

I don't want to ask a leading question. I don't want to give her a cop-out. But I'm itching with the desire to address the murder. Rene's murder. He did this, right? He's the only gangster in this story. The only one capable of putting his hands around a knife or a gun and aiming it at another person. Even at my basest temperament, I can't even deny a cup of tea without feeling some kind of remorse. I don't have it in me to kill. No drug can rewire me to be brutal.

"He's got a penchant for this. Mhm. This is his favorite game..." she continues, her focus drifting away from my expression and burrowing in her own thoughts. Her tale. "They warn you about 'im before you go to The Pup. I was heading out one night—I love a drink, but don't we all?—and a neighbor pulled me aside. He says, 'Where you off to, little lady?' And I says, 'The Pup, of course.' He just clicked his tongue at me. 'Uh uh. No you're not. That Rene Bordelon... I ain't ever see a woman leave his club. He ain't gonna do right by you, miss. Stay home.' I laughed it off, but when I got outside the doors I thought, 'Maybe I'll have a drink somewhere else,' and off to The Dog-House I went.

"Now, if my neighbor had meant prostitution, I don't think I'd be Rene's first choice, or even his second. I've aged out of that misery, and thank God for that. It's hard out here in New Orleans. Everybody gets tempted to put themselves in a position like that... their neck on the line for a little bit of cash. Just enough to tide you over... get some groceries. Anyway... that life is behind me, now. So the only other thing he could mean is murder. At least, that's what I assume. I never did ask him to clarify. I took his word—The Pup is just no place for a woman. But then I discovered you and your trumpet playing and I thought, 'Hell, if he can go in there with a brave face, then so can I.' Nothin' did happen to me. But to you... I'm so sorry, my boy.

"For murder, there is a place these gangsters like to go. When you leave my building, and you keep walkin' down the alley, you'll eventually find yourself in a clearing. It looks nice at first, but the deeper you get into it, the more these gnarly, twisted trees crop up. The ground gets wet and soupy. Suddenly, you're knee-deep in the treacherous waters. An alligator is much more troublesome than a man. And that's why they dump their bodies there. Mhm. Nobody's got the wherewithal to go huntin' through them waters. Anyone discarded there won't be found. Either the mud or the gators will take 'em. That's how Rene keeps gettin' away with it. By the time the police get the courage to search the backwaters it's too late."

Angela scoots her chair back and leaves the table once more, teacup in hand. It's only now that I notice the flask on her counter. Right beside the sugar and milk. I watch as she lights the flame beneath the kettle, opens another bag of tea, and pours in a healthy serving of sauce. She did say she likes drinking... I should have paid attention to the lilt in her cadence. The subtle slur toward the end of a sentence. She's holding her composure but there are still fissures in the facade.

"I don't know why he does this, if that's what you're wondering," she says, turning to face me with her back resting on the counter. "I'd be wondering the same. Hell, sometimes I spend hours thinkin' about it. He's definitely only after women, but they pose no threat to his business, or his hustle. He could pimp 'em but he doesn't. No... he just takes 'em out to the swamps and disposes of 'em. Guess you can't always explain a man's hatred for women. It's just in their nature. Problem is he's got the time and money to do away with as many women as he pleases. Tuh... I suppose he found a new way to spice up his game. Getting you involved."

I mull this over. "So you think he killed Telula, and now he's framing me?"

"If that's what you think I'm saying."

Whenever I ask for specifics she dodges the question. The potential culpability. Why share any information with me at all if she doesn't want to be responsible for the outcome? It's not like I can do much with this. It may ease the burden of curiosity on my brain, but it doesn't absolve me of sin in a court of law.

"Why are you telling me this?" I ask, my frustration surmounting, overpowering my respectability. She laughs, though. She isn't bothered. Maybe the alcohol has softened my language.

"Because, boy. I don't want my favorite musician rottin' in jail. I don't want innocent men taken off the streets. Maybe I'm just a bored old lady looking for some action, and my nosy ears got the best of me. But that don't mean I can't help you. Nothin' needs to be in it for me."

"But what am I meant to *do* with this?"

"Go to the swamps. Find what you're looking for."

"I don't know..." I look out the living room window. The sun is setting, the sky a marvelous shade of pink. I wish I could enjoy the evening, allow the magic of the environment to sweep me off my feet. I've always reckoned myself to be a romantic. Perhaps that's why this journey is so jarring—it's the opposite trajectory I saw for myself. The opposite of how I view the world.

"Stay the night. Rest up. Head out in the morning." She fills her cup with boiling water. She doesn't return to the table. This is her way of telling me to pack up for the evening. "I'll show you to your room, give you dinner in about an hour, and then you'll get some shuteye. Okay?"

"Okay," I say, without really thinking about it. I can't turn down a place to lay my head. I can't turn down a hot meal. I need my energy more than I need another fight.

She begins to walk away, and when I don't immediately follow, she shoots me a glare that says, *Come on, kid.* So I get up, and trail behind her through a narrow hallway. The walls are lined with family photographs, the picture frames extending too far out from the walls. I feel like my cheeks are grazing the glass on either side. When we get to the end I see a series of doors and rooms. She hooks a left and opens the door on the farthest wall.

The guest room reminds me of my place in that dingy hotel. A plain cot and ancient fixtures are all that's there. The window is small, high up, and lined with metal bars. She notices me staring at them and assures me this isn't a trap. I guess I have to believe her, or accept that perhaps being trapped in her apartment is preferable to being trapped in a New Orleans police station. At least here she offers me food and drink.

"I'll be back for you," she promises. And with that, I am alone.

***

I wake up to the sound of knocking. Startled, I throw off the blankets and scramble to my feet. "It's me! It's me..." that Creole voice coos. *Angela.* I'm in Angela's apartment. I must've passed out the moment my head touched the pillow. I didn't expect to get so comfortable. But the room is warm and cozy, my belly full of herbs. I drifted off without hesitation.

The doorknob squeals as she enters the room. She's holding a tray loaded with two plates and a giant glass of water. I accept it greedily, snatching the tray and sitting on the edge of the bed. My fork dives into a pile of mashed potatoes before I can even utter a "thank you." Angela doesn't seem to mind. She chuckles as she exits, softly closing the door behind her. Maybe I've been unkind to her. Who can blame me for assuming the worst, though? I don't think she could. I think she'd understand.

I don't taste the food as it briefly meets my tongue. I swallow before I've chewed most of my meal. I'm ravenous. A man eating his last supper before he's sent to the electric chair. Angela may not have a reliable narrative, but she does have the decency to give me a proper sendoff. Even if she's wrong about the swamps, I owe it to her to search them. I gather I can't stay here more than a night—just like Lenny, she's not interested in hiding a fugitive. Rumors fly fast in a small building. It's only a matter of time before I'm caught here, and she's too old to go down with me.

I've eaten too fast and now my stomach is bloated and angry. Or perhaps the thought of finding Telula's body floating in dirty swamp water has triggered my loss of appetite. I'm dreading tomorrow. I don't want to be back in the world. Even without the alligators, being spotted by a cop or a narc is always a possibility. I have to decide if staying in New Orleans is worth this—I could always flee the city, no? I can go back home, reunite with my family, and come up with a game plan. I can weigh my options with a roof over my head—clear my name or move elsewhere in the country. America is a big enough place to get lost. I can still take up my music in a different city—I bet the police haven't heard about me in Hollywood or New York. I can become an actor, let them paint me in different skin tones and hairstyles and watch myself transform every night on stage or in the pictures. I can lead an anonymous life away from this chaos. I don't need to be in New Orleans. I can run away. I can...

Chapter 7

Angela doesn't knock on my door again. She didn't come to collect my dinner tray in the middle of the night. I don't mind, though, as I shovel the scraps of food into my mouth. I fell asleep shortly after I gorged on food and woke up at the first hint of sunlight. I suspect it's seven o'clock. Birds chirp outside the window. If I didn't know any better I would take the serenity as a positive sign—but there's always a beautiful calm before the storm.

I rifle through the dresser in the room for a fresh set of clothes. I opt to leave a note on the bed informing Angela of the articles I've taken, and that one day I'd like to come back and repay her. I owe her, not just for her hospitality, but for her support—she watched my shows with a loyalty I do not deserve.

I quickly wash my face in the bathroom sink—the scratches are only slightly faded. The loose skin around the cuts is less apparent, replaced by a pink hue that radiates heat to the touch. Irritated, but not angry. The blood has dried and grown dark. It almost blends in with my skin, now. From a distance, I don't look as mangy and frightening. I slip the clean clothes over my aching limbs, and enjoy the momentary bliss of soft cotton on my ribs. It's only a matter of time before these pristine items are once again marred by the horrors that await me.

When I leave the apartment, Angela is nowhere to be seen. She probably wanted it this way—stayed in her bedroom as she heard me rustling around. Perhaps the alcohol knocked her out, and she'll remain in a comatose state until noon. Regardless, I'm alone as I make my exit.

***

Clouds roll in quickly, casting their bleakness over the once vibrant Sun. I guess it's better that the heat isn't beating down on me. I follow Angela's directions to a clearing. No buildings, no roads, no people. Nothing but tall, yellow grass. The arid environment dried out every weed and flower. The earth crunches and flakes beneath my feet. I don't understand why people love the summer—the humidity makes my bones ache. My skin is simultaneously greasy and unquenchable. Worst of all, nature dies. Some may say it's the winter that drives away the beauty of trees and rivers, but summer has that peculiar way of destroying a landscape. The brightness and warmth should mean all things glow and grow, but the world has never looked so barren. A wasteland of corpses.

It reminds me of Telula. It's my fault for building a version of her in my mind so far removed from reality. She was the sunshine that corroded my earth, turned it to dust. She hid behind her pretty face, her plausible victimhood, but her tongue was just as venomous as Rene's. That is, if I believe Angela; if I believe Lenny. Part of me wants to cling to my idea of her, my pathetic concoction. Why not? She might be dead, anyway. The thought makes me want to keel over, fall to my knees, and spew. I want to hate her. I do. I can't work through this mystery with rose-colored specs on. But what's the point in maliciously thinking of a dead woman? There's always the chance that I killed her, too.

I know Angela wants to absolve me of any wrongdoing, she's got the same issue as I—she sees me as a better person than I probably am. She wouldn't tell me anything particular about Telula and Rene, and them staying behind at the bar while I somehow trekked my way home in a blackout state doesn't make sense. I had to be escorted home. Whoever took me back to my room is either my attacker or my victim. It could have been self defense... They came at me with a gun so I found a knife and swung at them. That knife wasn't mine but maybe they had it on them. Why they would try to kill me—either of them—is still beyond my grasp.

Why would Rene kill Telula? I know I don't have a motivation, and drug-fueled rage doesn't ring true for me, but what about Rene? From what I gather, they were much closer than the club owner and singer. They were something else—partners in crime, partners in finances, and possibly romantic partners. The theory that he murdered her out of jealousy doesn't hold water when I apply the knowledge of their collusion to that evening—Rene intentionally brought me to Telula, and Telula knew he was going to do just that. They both sought me out—I wasn't a secret affair for Telula to hide.

Maybe Telula was stealing greenbacks from him. I was obviously bewitched by her, and my naivety made me a perfect decoy. I would have no objection to being set up, because I wouldn't be smart enough to catch on before it was too late. He swindled me with ease. A gangster may not like his girl running around behind his back, but he really doesn't like his money being fucked with. Telula probably got greedy—she saw how much The Pup was making and decided her pay wasn't fair. Rene promised her riches and the most she got was a shared bed with a grotesque man. Even if she loved him, he wasn't living nearly as nicely as he had claimed. A man like that doesn't know what real luxury is. She got sick of being under his thumb, of having to look at his gaudy wallpaper and clothes, and decided she needed better for herself. So she started rifling through drawers and suitcases and pocketing cash to one day make a break for it.

The clearing gives way to a line of trees on the horizon. Just as Angela said. The branches hang low, their dark green leaves creating a curtain before the swamp. It's as if they're masking the stage as it's being prepped. What horrors await me? The trunks are seemingly rotten, but nature has a way of sustaining itself in harrowing conditions. A swamp is no place for a human, and the brush states that clearly with its appearances.

The ground squelches now—a sign that water flows through these parts. I don't hear a gentle ebb, though. I don't detect the serenity of a pond or creek. No, the waters here are quiet. Waiting. They know that noise is the greatest indicator of prey. I am a lamb walking into a lion's den. The monsters that lurk here are laughing as I enter their lair.

The only bright side to crossing the threshold is the length of the tree branches—they lift, giving my eyes an intelligible lay of the land. The grass disappears into the roots of bushes. The bushes are difficult to pass—I can't find my footing. I'm continuously tangling my legs in the webs of sticks and leaves. The sun only filters through the breaks in trees, and even then, their radiation only highlights the horrid parts of the swamp—mosquitoes buzz in the yellow flares, snake scales reverberate the glare, sending it shooting back into my eyes. Even in the daylight, the swamps are nightmarish. I wish I was home.

As I near the water, I think about what body I might find, if I find a body at all. What if it's Rene's? I just assumed he was untouchable, but he's not a big man. He could be easily overpowered, even by a woman. If he had been lured into my room, he would have been without the protection of his bodyguards—he's always accompanied by at least one large man. Their shoulders are more expansive than Rene's entire body. If he was under the impression he would be alone with his woman, he would have shooed them away. Why would they think something bad would happen to him? Though, why he'd travel to an incapacitated man's hotel room is to be questioned. Maybe Telula offered him a chance to show her what a delicate man he can be—help a friend and he'll be rewarded.

He dropped me in my bed and advanced on her, hoping to claim his prize earlier than promised. That's when she reached for her knife, nestled tightly in her corset, and slit his throat. He may not have been an imposing man while he was alive, but I doubt she could drag his limp ligaments into an elevator and out the building. His bodyguards may have been the ones to tip the police off, though. They realized their boss was missing hours too late—my hotel was the last place they knew he'd been.

What am I supposed to do with the body? Do I stay with it until help comes? Angela said law enforcement rarely comes looking for the dead, but Rene is higher on the food chain than Telula. He would receive a search party. What would I say when they found me? I'm staking my claim to the evidence? I submit this corpse to the jury? Won't I look guiltier due to my proximity to the body? Why else would I be in the swamps, if not to dump my enemy and pray they never be seen again? My heart sinks lower in my chest—this was a fat headed idea.

I would turn back now, but my calves are already deep in the water. If I can't use this body to clear my name, I may as well ease my conscience. Perhaps it's more important that I have all the details for myself—I'm the only person I have to answer to. I'm the only person who's opinion on my lifestyle matters. If I go to prison, at least I'll go with every piece of the puzzle in place. No more questions to haunt me. The swamp water is dark, though. Brimming with algae and strange plants, nothing beyond the surface is visible.

I look up at the sky—cloudless and grim, for I cannot use any of its brightness to highlight my path. My legs slosh through the reservoir, and I cringe at every ripple I create. The beasts of this land were bred to respond to noise. The water is up to my thighs now. Soon it'll be grazing my shoulders, touching my ear lobes. If I'm nearly submerged, I'll have restricted movement and a lesser surveillance of the area. But the only way to uncover the truth is to keep pushing forward—to go deeper into the abyss, and hope I come out alive. I make my choice.

Soon, my feet lift off the mud, my body becoming buoyant in the lake. I'm not a great swimmer but I put what I know into practice—kick with the legs, spread with the arms. Half-circles. The realization dawns on me too late—how will I find my way back? At what point will I lose my sense of direction? The swamps are riddled with channels and ponds and forks in the road. Of course this is the perfect place to discard human remains—it's impossible to survey the entire area.

The skin on my hands is pruning—my palms are wrinkled like an ocean's wake. I'm parched from the exercise, the temperature of the swamp doing nothing to ease my heat. The sun wanes—I know my time is coming to an end. And then my hand connects with something—at first I think it's grass, but when I shake my wrist, it doesn't unlatch. Odd. I have to stop swimming for a moment, hovering in place as I attempt to free myself. I hate being a sitting duck. The more I try to unravel myself, the tighter the peculiar rope grips me. My heart rate climbs. I emit small gasps of desperation. *Calm down, Mo. It's nothing serious. Calm. Down.*

That's when I notice how soft the material is. It's not simply coated in the minerals and sludge from the swamp. It's something *else*. I grasp the strands and pull them to the surface. Hair. It's human hair. I'm mildly repulsed, but this is what I was searching for. I keep tugging, and soon the back of her head floats. Then her arms and legs. Face down in the bayou, I don't recognize her. The dress is orange and dotted—the fabric is vibrant enough to denote a recent passing. This could be her. This could be Telula. I can't apprehend the garment but my senses aren't reliable anymore. I can't be certain that what I remember of that night is true. I should turn the body over. Examine her features.

I take a deep breath. The Sun is setting soon. I can tell by the shadows cast on the swamp by the overhanging trees. How has time eclipsed so suddenly? I have to see her. It's the part in every story where the hero makes a grave mistake—he touches fire. He takes too much. He goes where he knows he shouldn't.

But just like them, I am tempted by my lack of choice. To look is to unlock a future not previously available to me, for better or for worse. I roll her over.

I instinctually move to cover my eyes but my fear is disrupted—I don't know this woman. *Fuck. I don't know this woman.* Fuck! I want this to be over. I'm exhausted from running. I'm burnt from all the anxiety. I can't live like this. I don't want to. I'm apologetic for my outrage—this woman deserves to be mourned. To have a proper burial. Instead she has me, whining over her watery grave. She's not the victim I was hoping to find. She is useless to me.

I'm not going to hold out hope any longer. Telula and Rene are not in these swamps. It might be my sensitivity, but I swear I hear tails and jaws cutting through the waters all around me. The alligators are circling, deciding when to encroach. When to attack. I search the deceased woman's body for anything that might tell me her name. Her dress has a secret pocket on the left side, but instead of a wallet or papers, it's filled with rocks. Whoever brought her here disposed of her poorly—if I hadn't disturbed her slumber, somebody or something would have. A low tide, perhaps, would expose her flesh to the elements. Is there more grace in drowning or floating through the bayou? Should I sink her and ensure she never be disrupted again, or do I set her free, giving her the chance to be found?

The sneer of a gator. That unmistakable huff of their nostrils. I abandon her body. I feel queasy doing it. Cowardly. My mind is perhaps playing tricks on me, leading me to my greater desire by falsifying noises in the wind. But I won't tempt fate a second time—I cross the lake once more. I keep my arms and legs close to my body. I maintain tiny gestures.

I move slower but create fewer cracks in the atmosphere. It's better to move silently than it is to move quickly. I retrace my steps as best I can. I only pray I can recall these last hours with more precision than I have been able to remark upon the previous night.

The water disintegrates. It collapses from my neck, to my waist, to my knees. I am standing once again, the threat of reptilian teeth clasping onto my chest a distant memory. I can see my way out from here. It's all coming back. Let's hope it stays this way.

Chapter 8

I'm almost at the clearing when the cops arrive. The night has settled in the sky, now. Navy blue prevails. Crickets have come out of hiding to chirp in harmony. I'm soaked—my clothes are too heavy to stay on properly, the wetness is intensifying the chill in the air. I hold my jaw shut as I stealthily exit the swamp—I don't want the cops to hear my teeth chattering.

At first I thought they could help me, mistaking them for some innocent passersby looking to go for an evening stroll. There was a single flashlight—a man and a dog—and not a word to be uttered. I hid in the bushes as I contemplated my plan—I wasn't going to throw myself in front of him and expect to be rescued. I'm not injured or dehydrated, just uncomfortable and tired. I'm glad I sat and evaluated him—shortly after I spotted him, more bulbs lit up behind him. I almost walked into an ambush with my arms raised and my eyes wide.

I worry that the dog will sniff me out—the only human scent in this forest—but it seems to be on a tight leash. It doesn't stray from its owner. Could this search be for the woman? Was she a high-powered individual? I may not be well-versed on the political and social landscape of New Orleans, but a woman in charge is always a cause for gossip. Or perhaps Angela sent them after me—they tracked my whereabouts down to her place. Eyewitnesses pointed fingers in exchange for bribes. Poor Angela had to defend herself against their absurd claims. I wouldn't blame her if she told them I attacked her just to protect herself. Then again, my penchant to assume the best of others has failed me time and time again. Maybe she lied about my name not being printed in the papers and saw an opportunity to collect some easy cash. At least she had the courtesy to give me a head start.

Once the policemen are in the dense brush, I crawl out of my hiding spot and into the tall grass. I remain on all fours through the first half of the open space—there's always a chance a cop lingered behind, or another is on the way. If someone looks in this direction, they'll quickly spot me. The only man in a sea of withered grass. I don't take my chances of being spotted until I'm halfway to civilization. At this distance, I could evade anyone who clocked me. I get onto my feet and sprint.

The grass thwacks me in the face as I fight my way through, stinging the cuts on my cheeks. The rustling sounds deriving from the friction between my pants and the brush startles me. Even if I am not seen, I may be heard. My tread is announced, my location a sonic pulse. I have tunnel vision as I run—the only object of my focus are the buildings coming into view. I'll dip into one for shelter, for a place to calculate my next move, if there are any moves to make at all. I have never been one for chess, but now I understand my inability to foresee my enemy's method of destruction has been my biggest blind spot. When I am betrayed or found, I never see it coming. It never crosses my mind until I'm in the throes of it.

The simplicity with which I escape the clutches of the police sends a chill down my spine—nothing good ever comes easy. I'm out of the field and headed toward a lone building—there's a sign above the door but it's not illuminated by neon piping. In the darkness it's hard to make out the hand-painted lettering. But a light is on outside this windowless tavern—I'll walk through the door and brace myself for whatever's on the other side.

Wind howls through the barren roads. I look over my shoulder to make sure I'm not being followed or watched. I definitely didn't return to Angela's neighborhood—I must have wandered much further than I thought. I'm just glad I managed to clamor my way back to civilization. A lucky break.

I reach the building and listen for any activity inside. The walls are windowless—there is nothing useful to help me determine what's going on inside, if anything's going on at all. I pray they aren't closed. I take a deep breath and pull the handle. It unlatches, and as the door widens its mouth, the sound of music slowly dribbles out into the night air. Jazz. The sweet, sweet melody of jazz.

I smile for the first time in days as I cross the threshold. I don't mind the dingy carpets or the poorly-patched walls. I don't mind the stench of cigarettes and cocktails. I am enamored with the steady pulse of the kick drum, the spontaneous, yet calculated crescendo of the piano. I perk my ears up at the saxophone, taking the lead as the player becomes inspired by his fellow musicians. It's all so invigorating. Maybe I won't survive my predicament. Maybe it's only a matter of time before I'm caught, once and for all. I've exhausted all my contacts, lost my bedroom and my anonymity. Perhaps I should indulge in one final night of freedom—jazz and a drink, an artist's dying wish.

Much like The Pup Café, the décor is rundown and dirty, speckled with years of dust and grime, but there's something charming about this place. Something earnest. As I enter the club space, I feel a welcoming presence—people are gathered around the stage, silently bobbing their heads along to the beat. The bartender watches wistfully. Noise is kept to a minimum—nobody wants to disrupt the music. The booths lining the back of the room are blackened—trails of smoke emanate from these dark corners. It's obvious that gambling and prostitution is taking place, but then, like Angela said, we all have to do things we're not proud of in order to make a living. I can hear the faint shuffle of cards, the plodding of coins on tables. I can hear broads feigning their deepest, sexiest voices for their potential clients. Bead curtains rattle together as men are led into a private space.

I turn my attention back to the bartender. Feeling curiously courageous, I approach him, the water in my stompers squelching with every step. He engages eye contact before I can place my hands on the counter. We stare at each other silently—he's waiting for me to order, I'm waiting to gauge his attitude. It's a stalemate. I guess I'll go first. I guess I'll be honest.

"Is there anywhere I can wash up?" I ask.

I assume he'll kick me out—despite the criminal activities taking place within the vicinity, my atrocious appearance is more alarming than any hive of gangsters. No man is supposed to walk around looking the way that I do. I am signaling to everyone my lack of self-respect. What owner would entertain my business?

"Yeah," he says curtly.

To my surprise, however, he leaves his post behind the bar and motions for me to follow him. I trail behind him as he pushes into a room with an EMPLOYEES ONLY sign etched into the door. They couldn't afford proper materials so they took a knife to a plate of wood. I half-chuckle at the sight. I respect the ingenuity. The refusal to give up. The back room is nothing more than two lockers, a stout bench, and faucet with a bucket over a drain. He opens a locker and presents me with the contents: a black T-shirt and a pair of khaki dress pants. "These look about your size," he says.

He shoves them into my chest, my mind too shocked by the generosity to tell my arms to accept the garments. He leaves without another word—the rest is self-explanatory. Fill the bucket with water, soap up, and get changed. Am I still in New Orleans?

***

I throw my old clothes in the trash on my way out. They're laced with weeds and algae, their sleeves and legs buried by the muck that clings to the crusty fabric. I don't need those anymore. I've transformed into a different man—my second metamorphosis in a single day. I'm no longer trying to acquire nobility or class, I'm no longer trying to appease those who wouldn't hesitate to turn their noses up at me.

I sit at the counter and the bartender begins pouring me a drink. I don't even have to tell him what I want—he slides me a whiskey, neat. Tears well in my eyes, the hot liquid stinging the skin on my lids. I don't play it off—I'm done masking myself. "Thanks, man," I say, a crack in my voice.

He shrugs. "What's your name?"

I think for a moment. "Maurice."

"Everybody's welcome in my club, Maurice." He drops his gaze and continues to dry off freshly washed glasses with a rag.

I pay attention to the stage—a duo is performing, two brass instruments battling for dominance. It appears the talent is rotating. I look around the club and notice a poster plastered to the wall: Tonight is open-mic night. Anyone can play—the stage is fair game.

I sip my whiskey and allow the liquor to fill my belly with its heat. The warmth is serene, pleasurable, homely. In all my regrets, I forgot how much I love jazz. How much I love being on stage. I did come here for a reason, and I can scold myself for my high hopes and lack of awareness surrounding the truth of the world, but that doesn't diminish my passion for music. My zest for adventure. I've spent the last two days bemoaning my situation, feeling sorry for myself and chastising my inability to have foreseen it. But that hasn't gotten me anywhere. It hasn't helped me in my interactions with others. My nihilism hasn't led me to any clues. Perhaps none of this would have happened if I had never moved to New Orleans, but ruminating on a past I can't return to won't change the present. A restless life, albeit a safe one with my parents, would have been just as disappointing as this one.

I'm drifting toward the stage. I don't remember getting up from my seat. I've left my drink on the counter. The glass was empty, anyway. There's a lull in the music as people scan the crowd, wondering who will volunteer to get up there next. I'm already up the stairs before I can give this a second thought. I see a drum kit, piano, and trumpet splayed on the black tile. My boldness wanes as I pick up the shiny instrument—am I fostering a self-fulfilling prophecy by engaging in a final performance? I run the pads of my fingers along the smooth metal. Press them firmly into the material. Grip the neck of the trumpet firmly in my hands. I need to do this. For me. I'm so concerned with regrets and here I am facing my biggest one—to die with my music or without it. I choose to die with it.

The audience is tranquil as I take in a deep breath. I hear the particles of air rushing into my lungs, the anticipation in the atmosphere. I hear the slight clinks of glasses as people swirl their ice-filled cocktails, the nervous scratching of nails on skin. I bring my lips to the mouthpiece. The first note comes out gloriously. Crisp. Pitch perfect. My consciousness melts away as I fade into a song. The melody isn't predetermined. The notes never spent a moment floating around in my brain before this. They come out effortlessly, their progression bittersweet. The crowd remains taciturn—I take it to mean they're enthralled. What's wrong with hoping for the best?

I wasn't a schnook for believing Telula to be someone she's not. For believing she was an honest musician just trying to make her way in a big city. We all want to map our experiences onto others, to find community in our sameness. Hell, I'm only here because I saw my passions reflected in Duke Ellington and Louis Armstrong. I yearned to be surrounded by artists who saw the world the same way I did. Who could mentor me, commune with me, and offer me valuable lessons. I wasn't chasing a life of fame and glory, but of humble connections and relationships. My ire with New Orleans is not the seedy underground or the mafia men running gamuts all over town, but the refusal of others to bond with me. To see me as human. As someone worthwhile. They're so concerned with their own survival they've forgotten that a life devoted to fear is not truly living. The *what ifs* have led them to isolation, have forced them to turn away friendships in favor of malignant independence.

Telula could have arrived in New Orleans with the same attitudes as I, only to be faced with a similar dejection. She, however, divulged her nastiness, stooping to the level of Rene and his followers. If confronted, she would probably give me a long spiel about how she had no choice. I've been saying that about myself, too. *I just didn't have a choice.* That's too easy of a way out—too easy to shirk my burdens and place them onto someone else. I am not a defeated man. I will not let the malice of others hinder my growth, hinder my prospects.

The tune I'm playing shifts—the slightly somber melody becomes an angry cacophony. The audience adds their murmurs to the ambiance. The symphony of hushed voices and drink orders inspires my direction. I haven't felt this electric in months—The Dog-House was stifling me, encouraging me to stick to a particular tempo and keep the preferences of the crowd in mind. But here, I am uninhibited. I am not ashamed of my choices. I am not repressing my whims. I am a man untethered. Why can't I apply this emotionality to my life? Why must I continue to allow Rene to walk all over me? To make me a villain?

I've been doubting myself—I'm just a boy with too much on his plate. I bit off more than I can chew. All that nonsense. I've been letting Rene win by omission—I may not have a bountiful life but it's still worth fighting for. I'm young. I'm talented. I have the world at my fingertips. I can't let a pedestrian gangster and his wannabe singer chase me away. I am not a murderer, and I refuse to let that bum rap tarnish my name.

The trumpet vibrates between my palms as I hit high note after high note. Claps have begun to erupt around the room. It's not a unanimous cheer—just enough anxious hands itching to announce their enthusiasm. I know that I have reached the end of my song—it's a guttural feeling. Indescribable. I put down the instrument gently, a peculiar juxtaposition to my previous rage, as the echo of my last blare continues to ring throughout the club. I'm panting as I step back, finally able to evaluate the room with clear eyes. Some guests are standing on their feet, eyes fixed on me. Others are whispering to their partners. The gambling in the back has momentarily paused—I'm an outsider who's not only disrupted their evening, but demanded their attention. But they applaud—I am a welcome interference.

For once, I feel like I belong. I am not the shiny new toy for clubs to take advantage of and bolster to sell tickets. I am not the intruder in someone's backyard, or the unwelcome body in someone's bed. It may require some grit to make my way through the jazz scene, but there are treasures at the end of the rainbow. I don't need to succumb to the foibles of others, or accept my measly prizes. I will once again varnish the name that Rene stole from me. I will set myself free of this curse, once and for all.

Chapter 9

The night air is refreshing on my brand new skin. I feel unsoiled. Polished. There is still wonderment and beauty to be had during times of turmoil. I asked the bartender to point me in the direction of my hotel, and he put me on a straightforward path. It's strange to have lived somewhere for so long and still not be able to map it out. To understand it. Had I wandered out here alone, without any such guidance, I would have found myself lost and standing on someone's doorstep, begging for instructions. I set off down the road, and brace myself for what's to come.

The streets are eerily empty tonight. The weather is marvelous, conducive to a night of barhopping and dancing in the town square. Musicians are more than likely bouncing from club to club, supplying the score to an evening in New Orleans. But the crowds aren't following suit. I yearn to maintain the optimistic outlook of my epiphany, but the unsettling nature of the barren roads is causing me to second-guess myself. Nobody stops partying in this town, which begs the question: *What horrible thing happened?*

Time is of the essence, but I fear that if I bring my gait above a fast walk I'll attract trouble. I know how gossipy these people can be, and now that they're viewing me from their apartments, looking down on me with trepidation and too much time on their hands, they'll be ready to consider me a threat. I have to be as calculated as Rene was the night he removed Telula's corpse from my room—surveilling the area without being obvious; hiding suspicious activity through overt casualness. If I want to outsmart my enemies I have to temporarily play their games.

***

The hotel looks the same as always—no cops are loitering around the perimeter, the usual group of hookers are hanging by the front doors, and most of the lights are on in the squat building. The building is always illuminated, the bathrooms always packed, but the rest of the hotel is empty. A dead zone. I know when I walk through the halls to my room I will be alone. That certainty brings me solace. I hold onto it as I unlock the back door and step inside. I hold onto it as I slowly scale flights of stairs. The concrete absorbs the sound of the soles of my feet landing on each stair and reverberates it throughout the vicinity. Nobody ever greets me during my climb. Nobody passes me. I exit at my floor and am greeted by another barren wasteland.

Sconces line the walls; the flames burning inside them dull and barely functional. My room isn't far from the stairwell, and I can see from a distance that nobody has been posted outside my door. There are no markers of someone having been there, either. No chair, or desk, or food crumbs. The only noticeable change is the yellow tape smeared across my door. CAUTION, the tape reads. My mouth dries at the notion of a crime scene investigation taking place in my room. They must have torn it apart, looking for clues in the seams of my jackets and trying to piece together my origins in order to make sense of my heinous rage. I wonder what they considered remarkable evidence.

I press my ear to the door before turning the knob—perhaps personnel have gathered inside to workshop the particulars. They might be doing exactly what I'm here for—to figure out the murder. Figure out who did it. My attempts to rope other people onto my team have gone belly up—I can only rely on myself now to get the job done. I don't detect footsteps or furniture moving. I can't discern voices or catch the scent of cigarette smoke. Hopefully, nobody has set foot in this room since the morning it was discovered. I need time alone with the evidence.

I swing open the door and my blood drains. The room has been tidied. The bed is stripped, though the pool of blood on the mattress could not be done away with—some evils can't be scrubbed clean. The weapons have been removed from the scene, and in their place are haphazard chalk outlines meant to evoke their prior positions. Even the walls are nicer than how I left them—some dried stains remain spackled on the wallpaper and carpet, but there's been an attempt to erase all evidence. *Shit.* How am I supposed to go through the motions of that fateful morning when nothing is in its proper place?

I close the door behind me and lock it—I don't want to chance an unexpected invasion. Perhaps this is my first clue—the knob only locks with a key. And I have it. The only other copy would be at the front desk—it wasn't given to the police, though. The room was open, save for some warning tape. That means I was the one to enter the room last. Or, someone made a copy of my key. That would be a simple task for a well-connected man like Rene—he's no stranger to counterfeits. It's possible that he drugged me, slipped the key out of my pocket at the club, had a new one fashioned while

Telula kept my sauced ass occupied, and returned the original to me without my noticing. Considering I was blacked out, this task would have been all the more easy. Telula wouldn't have to wave her hands in front of my face or press her lips to my skin. She would just have to sit there and make sure I don't wander off.

I stare at the violated mattress, trying to bridge this train of thought to the murder itself, but the stench emanating from the bodily fluids just sitting there, watching me, brings me back to that morning. The horror. The anxiety. The knee-buckling nausea. I feel myself fading, my heart slipping into an irregular beat, my tongue swelling from the threat of bile. I throw an arm out and prop myself up against the wall—steady now. Take it easy.

I dart across the room to crack open a window—I need a breather, for the wind to carry out the vile odor. But as I trek across the floor, I notice the chalk outlines of the weapons. They always did strike me as strange—a gun *and* a knife? This murder was calculated—from the disposal of the body, to the replication of the key and my forced comatose state, this wasn't a random event. Though it's always possible I hid the body and came back to my room for a nap, locking the door behind me. I know I don't have that evil within me. I am not culpable of this crime. I know enough to determine my innocence and the obvious truth—I am being framed for this killing.

Why would you stab and shoot someone? Slicing and serrating makes more sense for a murder so public—the walls of this hotel room are thin, there are ears always awake and listening, whether they are outside or right next door. Of course, using a gun would ensure a quicker, more accurate death. Rarely do people survive wounds from bullets, but a stab in the wrong place is the difference between life and death. A knife may not penetrate as deeply, may not kill as swiftly, enabling the victim to holler and scream for help. A shot to the head and our murderer is home free—all that would be left to do is wrap up the body and take it outside.

I guess Rene could have held his hand over Telula's mouth as he cut her to pieces, but he's not an overtly strong man. The adrenaline coursing through her veins would be enough to fight him off, especially if he only had one hand supporting his weight and suppressing hers. Then there's always the possibility that he had help—did a bodyguard stand outside the door, making sure nobody was alerted to the noise, to the struggle? Was another in the bed with him, pinning Telula down as she fought for her life? That may also explain the multiple weapons—a lackey carrying a gun accidentally dropped it in the shuffle. But it was placed so neatly beside my head—if it was intended that I be found with the evidence, there's no way that gun was left behind mistakenly.

The remnants of blood spatter reach all four corners of the room—this is consistent with neither weapon. If the victim had been shot, there would be cranial matter on the headboard. If the victim had been stabbed, the blood wouldn't have shot out of their body. Unless the murderer ran around the room, dipping their fingers into the open wound and painting it on the walls, the patterns just don't make sense.

If it was a crime of passion, perhaps I wasn't an intentional scapegoat; otherwise, why remove the body at all? If they wanted me to be found guilty, they would have left a rotting corpse in my room. There's no talking my way out of that.

No proving my irreproachability. Why give me a way out of this mess? A leg to stand on? No body no crime is a common philosophy in this town. And if he didn't bring the body to the swamp, where did he take it? Did he drop it in a garbage can on the street? Bring it back to The Pup Café and hide it under the floorboards? What sense would it make to keep her corpse, or to discard it in plain sight? The closer Telula is to the scene of the crime, the easier it is to have the fingers point back at him.

The stench hits me again, and I bolt to the window. Opening the latch, I throw my head out, taking heaping gulps of the clean air. The fumes are choking me out—I don't know how much longer I can stay here. The attack just doesn't make sense—it's erratic, brimming with indecision, riddled with as many mistakes as I've made in the last two days. It's the work of an amateur. Maybe Rene isn't as cunning as he's cracked up to be—he camouflages himself with his clothing, hoping they signal authority and competence. His veneer of prowess and domination is an elaborate hoax. The only thing he's ever succeeded at is his facade—without it, he's just another chump in a fedora, desperately trying to build an empire out of straw.

I dip my head back into the room and a wall of grief hits me. Death. There is death in my room. There is death because of me. I'm spiraling, the downward tumble an unstoppable force. I back myself into the corner, the mattress taunting me as I slide to the floor, knees to my chest. I cough and retch, the blood overpowering my senses, driving me mad. The particulars of Rene's ploy no longer distract me—I must come to grips with the murder that took place beside me. In a space that is supposed to be safe, regenerating, intimate. Somebody forced me to be complicit in violence against my will. How would I have reacted if I was awake? Would I have stopped the ordeal, or froze in terror? Is it better to have slept during the crisis or to have witnessed it?

The transgression of my sanctity has been but a dull drone in the back of my mind—irrelevant to the task at hand. But now that I'm here, affronted by the straits of the ordeal, I realize how disgusting it is that I was implicated in such an atrocious act. Even if I solve the murder, how will I cope with the violation of my body? How will I sleep at night with the stench of decay stuck to my nostrils? What if the event starts coming back to me? The further I am removed from the situation, the less effect the drug has on me, the more I may remember. I assume I was asleep but I could have been merely incapacitated—a paralyzed body ready for surgery, watching as the doctors slice open my numb belly and pull out my organs. I can clear my name but I can't reverse this horrifying experience—I can't make it go away from the depths of my unconscious. I have been permanently scarred, so selfishly, so callously.

I weep. I finally let myself weep. My shoulders bounce, my lungs shake, my lips fill with my own tears. I cry for all the times I couldn't before. For all the times I forced myself to put on a brave face and push forward. I miss my mother. I miss the way she strokes my cheeks and brushes away my sadness. I miss the way she shows affection with a warm meal. I miss going to my grandparents' farm with her, holding her hand as she introduces me to the goats and the cows, shows me how to plant a garden and fry an egg. She taught me how to take care of myself, to be a strong man. I miss being a child and not having to apply this knowledge yet, to know that independence is on the horizon, but today I can lean on my mother.

I miss my father, too. I miss hearing about the ocean. He would take me out on the boat sometimes, when he knew the sea would be calm. He would point into the abyss and have me guess which creatures were floating below, ducking underneath the boat and attempting to steal bits and pieces of his prey. I miss steering the ship—the road before me was crystalline and dancing, the destination uncertain, yet anything I wanted it to be. I was the king of the world for a moment. With my hands on the wheel, I could take us anywhere in the world. Of course I grew up to be a dreamer. I had an unfettered imagination that was merely coaxed into its full potential—between the music and the sea, I was destined to crave miraculous things.

And I miss the sticks. I miss the climate, the air. Everything was docile in comparison—the weather was humid, yet conducive to farming. The only garbage was the scraps we created. We could live for ourselves, even if that meant living humbly. I miss taking a stroll down the street, and coming across trees and animals instead of litter and piss. I miss having quiet places to hide in, to gather myself. I never considered myself to be a nature boy, but now that I've had my access denied, with only the dangerous swamps in proximity, I regret my lack of appreciation for the wilderness. Smog hurts the lungs, hurts the soul. I mourn my lost innocence, for it's something I can never get back.

As I whimper into my hands, my palms growing slick with the salty tears, the stench in the room becomes less accosting. It transforms into something familiar. Something on the brink of comforting. I sniff with vigor as I attempt to suss out the complexities in the odor. My spine tingles—I feel as though I'm onto something. I steadily get up—my knees crack as I straighten, as if my bones are resetting. The blood calls to me. It's the way the radio called to me. The way Telula did. The way I have been lured time and time again. It's a similar beg. A plea. I inch toward the mattress, behaving as if it might jump up and snap at me, or pull me into its clutches and smother me to death. It teems with energy—suddenly alive, the blood infiltrating the fibers as though it were filling veins. It has something to say. I can tell.

I timidly sink my hands into the springs and lean my ear down, my miniscule hair follicles grazing the fabric. With my nose close to the source of the smell, I have a striking feeling that something isn't human. My eyes grow crimson, like the pond of blood before me. I'm no longer afraid of the stain—it hasn't marred my spirit. It can't. That didn't come from a person. It didn't spill out of Telula's neck or Rene's stomach. This is the blood of an animal. It reeks of slaughterhouses and farms. Of my hometown. I would know this stink anywhere. Rene may think he has the upper hand, that he's too clever to be beat, but I'm not taking this lying down. I have a war to win.

Chapter 10

I stalk into The Pup Café with an assertiveness I didn't know I had. I'm not here to plead with Rene, to force his hand and take him to the police. I know I'm operating on a hunch—the scent is beastly, but that is not a quality I can prove. I tell the cops that ain't no human blood and Rene throws me under the bus—"Mo is a looney who got handsy with my girl one night. Don't believe a word he says." Now we're locked in a game of "he said, she said." I'm not going to bother engaging it on any level higher than this—I'm clearing my name with the people that matter. The people who will believe me—my patrons, my colleagues, my fellow musicians. Cops be damned, what's important now is sticking up for myself. Putting an end to Rene's charade in a way that matters to me.

A cello and hightop peter out as I enter the club. The two performers on stage share a puzzled look as Rene approaches them, a hand out as a signal for them to stop. The crowd is just as confused—some people keep dancing, even after the music has dissipated. Others murmur worriedly, their voices carrying throughout the dim expanse. The musicians are corralled off the stage—Rene's men lumber in behind him, picking the drum kit up piece by piece, disconnecting wires from microphones, stealing the stools out from under the entertainers.

"Thank you, fellas," Rene says into his mic. It's a personalized hunk of equipment—wrapped in gold and studded with diamonds, all probably fake, the microphone is just as gaudy as his outfit. His staple fedora is placed crookedly on top of his head. His cobra cane is tucked under his arm as he juggles the mic in one hand and a sheet of paper in the other. He dons an excessive fur jacket, the sleeves of which eclipse his arms and make his hands appear feeble. He's swallowed by the enormity of his costume. Of his ruse. "Thank you for your cooperation," he repeats.

The artists are stunned—they are not going of their own volition. They've been effectively kicked off their damn set. Jeers come from the back corners of the room—people are not enthused about this disruption. "Hey, I've got a song!" someone heckles from the depths of the audience.

"That's alright, we'll be getting back to our regularly scheduled program in a moment," Rene assures. "Let's settle down now." He motions for the crowd to zip their lips. People are so offended they actually comply. What is the matter with this man? The mere presence of him enrages me—should I wait to hear what he has to say, or should I storm the stage and make my accusations while the aura in the room is tense. Aggravated. Perhaps they'll be on my side while their spirits are low, their opinion of Rene tanking with each second he stands there busting their chops as though they were a group of kindergarteners.

"I have an urgent matter to discuss with you folks," he continues.

"Who cares?" comes another heckler.

"Bring back the band!" says another.

The audience resumes their normal volume, people pairing off to discuss the peculiar events. They paid for booze and blues—they don't want to be lectured by Rene. What does it matter to them that he's the owner of the club? That doesn't make him special. Not when they're drunk, at least. People always have more courage when their minds are partially impaired. I try not to worry about my own bender. I have absolved myself of that. I was drugged. I can't keep slipping back into that nightmare, because if I do I'll never break out of it. I'll never confront Rene. I grip my fingers into fists, allowing my nails to dig deep into my skin, to keep me alert. Present.

"You'll regret your words, I promise you that," Rene warns. People blow raspberries. Others laugh. Some even walk out the door. "Immature... tsk tsk. Some y'all never grow outta that."

He dramatically shakes his head as he pauses to consult his notes. The arrogance he displays is off-putting, even to his customers. Perhaps I overestimated his pull in this town—maybe his reach only extends to those on his level, of a similar status. He can intimidate other club owners and manipulate the police force, but he can't buy the affections of the public.

"It pains me to tell y'all that our beloved Telula is in the hospital—" Rene begins, before he is cut off by a series of shouts from the audience. The tide has turned—now they want to hear his announcement. The leering is in regards to her injury, and not his interruption. Telula has the hearts of the people. She was able to touch them in a way Rene never could. Is this another motivation? But wait... she's only injured?

"Yes, yes, I know, I know." He once again motions for the crowd to be silent. This time, they comply without resistance. I shift awkwardly in place—now an attack would be a violation. They would decry my presence, demand that I be removed from the premises. I'd be spitting on Telula's reputation, on her legacy. I can't do it now. *Fuck.* Have I missed my opportunity?

"Late Saturday evening, Telula was assaulted by a man. This man had been stalking 'er, waitin' for 'er after every show, knocking on 'er door in the middle of the night. Tuh... this guy was a real loser. Telula told us not to worry, though. She had a hang of it. We told 'er we would kick him out should we see him come to The Pup again, and she said 'no, no, no.' Silly girl. But I blame myself more than anything. I shoulda known better. I shoulda forced 'er to take my security, to never spend another night alone. I tried, fellas. I tried. But some things you just can't control. They say he drugged 'er right here in my Café... under my watchful eye..." Rene brings the back of his hand to his eye and rubs it as if to emulate crying. Pathetic chortling noises emanate from the speakers. What a fucking performance. What a show. I want to pounce—to jump on stage and wring my hands around his neck. Drain him of all the color in his face.

"Ah, man... it hurts my soul knowing this happened in my vicinity. It coulda happened while any one of ya's was watching. Probably didn't think anything of it. Nah, 'cause this was a handsome man. Real talented, too. He's just like our Telula in a lot of ways... perhaps that's what makes him such an unsuspecting perpetra'uh. I'm sermonizing, I know. I apologize." Rene takes a giant gulp of air. "He drugged 'er, offered to carry her home, and took 'er to his hotel instead. By the time we realized she was missing, it was too late. I dunno if I should say this next part... it's vile. Not right...."

Another dramatic pause as he waits for the crowd's reaction—he's imploring them to beg. To demand answers. He wants them to shout for him to continue his devilish rant. If only they knew the lies that were spewed by his tongue. If only they knew what conniving bullshit was behind his false melancholy. And Telula... she's alive? They're both alive? I don't know how to feel. I don't know how to make sense of it anymore.

"Telula was stabbed repeatedly. Reports are sayin' six or seven times. O'er and o'er again. Shit, man... I dunno how she survived. She's a lucky duckling, that one. Now y'all keep 'er in your prayers, 'cause she's fightin' for her life. Every last breath counts."

"Who did this to her?" someone hollers.

"I'll get to that, y'all believe me. He won't be gettin' off for this one, I'll tell you that," he responds. My ears boil as the obvious conclusion to this debacle draws near—Rene will name me and tarnish my reputation forever. If I don't end up in jail, I'll never work again. Not with the vitriol I'm about to receive. A claim like this will follow me for the rest of my life. There's no running away from it, not if I want to stay in the jazz scene, that is. And I do. He can't destroy me.

"Only a sick monster could—" Rene starts, but I'm already barreling toward the stage. Before anyone can stop me, I've hopped the steps and landed squarely in front of Rene. Even he doesn't have time to react—my fist is already in his face. I hear the crunch of his nose as my knuckles impact. He tumbles to the ground. I jump on top of his defenseless body and start wailing—I'm digging my own grave, yes, but I've had enough. One man can only take so much.

I've beaten Rene's face black and blue when his bodyguards finally pull me off. I kick my legs out, landing more blows to his torso as they tug me away. I won't stop flailing, so they drop my arms and pin me down. That's when I'm knocked out. Cold.

***

I come to in a liquor cellar. The dirt floor beneath my queasy legs is frigid, like I'm sitting on layers of snow and ice in the middle of January. My hands are asleep—that awful static radiating through my fingers. I try to flex them but they're stuck. *Fuck, I'm tied up.* I jolt forward and my body goes nowhere. I look down at my feet—they're bound together. I wince, my face scrunching, and I can tell I have a swollen cheek and a fat lip. My entire mouth aches as I curve it upward. I wish I could cup my injuries in my palm. I wish I could move. I crane my neck to look at the object holding me back—I'm strapped to a wooden barrel filled with ale. Though I know it's futile, I still try to free myself—maybe if I wriggle enough the ropes around me will magically untether.

I'm so caught up in my plight I don't even notice Rene sitting in a chair facing me. Nor do I notice his two bodyguards, standing with their hands clasped behind their backs, on either side of him. It's only when he chuckles that I pay attention to the source of the racket. I narrow my eyes as I gaze upon him—his face is entirely bandaged, save for his left eye. He looks ridiculous with gauze taped around his head. If he's meant to be menacing, he needs to do a better job of maintaining that appearance. He has his left leg resting on his right knee, his hand grasped firmly around his cane, and his fedora in the other. With his hair exposed, I detect the missing follicles along his scalp. His hairline is receding, his thick locks fading. He's an aging man trying desperately to appear as anything but.

"Mawh-reese," he says with his hammed up droll. Nothing about him is real, so why should I believe his accent, too?

"Rene," I spit back.

"Well, well. You figured it was me, eh?" He gets up from his seat and begins to pace. His lack of height does nothing to intimidate me. "That performance of yours did you no favors, I can tell you that."

"I don't need favors."

"Ah ah ah." He wags a finger at me. The sight is repugnant. "I'll tell you what you need. You're just a schnook who won't stop getting his hands dirty, what the fuck do you know?"

"Just tell me what you want from me." I'm tired of this charade.

"I don't *want* anything from you. I already have it. Took it. You have nothing left to give that I haven't stolen."

"So why am I here?"

"I dunno. You tell me. I was the one who got attacked, after all." He gestures to his mummified face.

I roll my eyes. "Big fucking baby. Can't take a punch."

"And you can't let sleeping dogs lie."

"What do you want from me?" I repeat, my words slow, and concise, a pause between each syllable.

He sighs. "If you insist on me reading you a story, I guess I'll have to oblige. Though I am tired from my hectic day, so, forgive me while I rest." He gets back in his chair, this time with his left leg extended, his lower back almost slipping into a slouch. "Listen, I know there are tales about me all over town. 'The Crook o' New Orleans,' they call me."

"I've never heard that one," I interject. I refuse to abide by his inflated ego.

"You don't know when to shut that trap, do ya?" He rolls his eyes at me, a childish dismissal, and continues. "Whether you heard the tales or not, I gotta reputation in this here town. I'm not one to be messed with, so they say. And though they'd be wrong to assume my malice, they're correct in their assertions of my veracity. See, I'm turnin' a new leaf. I wanna make this community bett'uh. I'm tired of lookin' out there and seeing boarded-up windows and foreclosure signs. I hate the damned tourists and the rich folk that move here for a weekend and decide there's nothin' of value left. This place used to be vibrant. Booming. You made greenbacks just by walkin' down the street and holding your hand out. Art was born here. That's what I believe. Bet you think the same thing since you came here, same as the rest of 'em. Same as our girl Telula."

He pauses to monitor my reaction, of which he receives none. I'm not going to show my hand this early. He raises his eyebrows, surprised—disappointed?—and sinks further into his seat. "When I started my business, I was an honest man. Sure I bought this building with my pimpin' money, but hey, we can't all have squeaky clean records. It was a different time, then. I didn't have to worry 'bout bills, 'bout profits or customers. Nothing of the sort. No... the people came to me, and they came willingly. I was so spoiled in my early days I never foresaw the depression. War changes things, though. And so did those greedy artists—Faulkner, Armstrong, King Oliver—they didn't stick around to save our city. Nah, even the ones who was born here up and left when things took a turn. They abandoned us. And you know what I got for it? Debt. A whole lotta it.

"But I'm a hustler. So I pull up my bootstraps and get to work. I turn things around—now I ain't no greenback maker, but I do alright for myself. I do alright for my girl, too. Telula's the whole reason I got my freedom back. She sings, and the people come. That is... until you started playin' at The Dog-House most every night. Shit... I haven't had competition like that in years. And I know what you're thinkin', 'Rene, there's always gonna be competition. Especially in music.' That may be true, but you posed a particular problem for me an' my bar. 'Cause you just kept playin' every damn night. Nonstop. Usually, we're able to stake a claim on a couple days during the week. Monday, Thursday, Friday... but not with you 'round. Nope."

"That's not my fault," I interject. "I'm contracted by The Dog-House."

Rene laughs. "That's a much bigger target, boy! Take down an entire establishment? Shit, I'll just go after the weakest link—their dolled up lil hillbilly obsessed with my girl. I watched you with your goofy moon eyes gawking at 'er every night, and this plan... well it fell right into my lap. Can't hate a gangster for playin' his games. Telula was sick of it, too. This town isn't big enough for two stars. Before you came 'round, she was gettin' offered side gigs for private shows. Sure, some of 'em were perverts looking to ogle her without me keepin' an eye out, but it was all 'er own money. Went straight to 'er pockets. With you in the picture, they lost interest.

"Broads... so easily persuaded sometimes. She already had the feelings I just gave 'er the push. It wasn't hard, though, to convince 'er to drug you. She was fine with that, but couldn't pull the trigger. Said she wanted to keep violence outta it. I says,

'Alright... but that don't get rid of him. He'll still be 'round, maybe just a little scared.' That got 'er thinkin'. So we concocted our own plan. A soft pill for 'er to swallow. We knew you was being put up by The Dog-House, so anything we did to you would fall back on 'em pretty quickly. Nobody wants to go to the club where they got their boys beatin' up our dear Telula. Now, I think a murder woulda been better. It probably would've drove you to the looney bin before the slammer, tryna deal with all that guilt. But hey, sometimes you gotta make concessions to get shit done. I still got you cockeyed, though. I got a few tricks up my sleeve.

"We use 'er to get to you. She drugs you and we mess up your room. Some pig's blood and a few weapons and you're in the shit. Gave an anonymous tip to the po-lice that mornin' and watched you scramble to get free. Granted, you got farther than I thought. Really hoped they woulda caught you by now, but I guess this works, too. I get to watch you go down." He laughs, pulls a cigarette out of his pocket, and lights it with ease. It's almost cool, but his attire ruins the suave movements.

"So, that's it? This is all over some crowd coverage on weeknights?"

"It's about my livelihood, you damn knucklehead!" He stands as he yells at me. Cigarette smoke forms a ring around his blazing ears.

"Get more performers, man. Easy fix. Hell, you could've had me and Telula singing together. You're just a fucking imbecile—you wanna act smart, like this was some elaborate scheme, but I'm still here. You ain't got shit on me. Just your nasty fucking mouth."

I can see the rage boiling under the surface, but he makes a concerted effort to mask it. Bury it down deep. I haven't said enough to justify him blowing up—he's just an insecure man with a short fuse. He knows just as well as I do that if he implodes, I win.

"No...." He turns his back to me. "You see, I'm going to give you a choice. You can either wait for the cops to arrive, or you can die. A slow, painful death, of course."

I laugh. I laugh and I laugh and I laugh. I can't stop it. I can't push it back down my throat. My lungs burn as I attempt to stop them from shaking, from gasping for air. I am helpless. In my state of shock, I have succumbed to my basest feelings. This is silly, is it not? Was I supposed to be shooting my opponents square in the forehead every time they crafted a riff better than mine? I know some people die for their art, and others kill for it, but Rene's not even the artist, and he couldn't coerce his muse to agree to such a bidding. He claims winning back his business was his utmost priority, and yet he failed to actually rid himself of the one person holding him back. This threat is nothing more than a longshot. A last resort. I'm not supposed to be here and he knows that. He's grasping at straws.

Rene grimaces at my hysterics. "Fine. Death it is. Fucking prick." He motions for the bodyguards to head out. He follows suit, his cobra cane held behind his back. The gemstone eyes stare at me. He cocks his head to speak to me, but he doesn't have the audacity to meet my gaze. "I'll be back for you when The Pup is closed. Then I will torture you. Mercilessly. I know you laugh. You don't take me seriously. But you won't find it funny when I chop off your arm and feed it to you. I mean business, Mawh-reese."

They enter into a hallway I can't see into. It's too dim. I'm too far away. And there are tears in my eyes. Tears that continue to flow when the door clanks shut behind them. Tears that roll down my cheeks for hours after they're gone. I'll be laughing in my grave, in awe of the pitiful man who called for my death.

Chapter 11

It takes a while, but the giddiness settles. I thought I would be more frightened than I am. The exasperation didn't transpire into another emotion. It simply faded. Gone. I have nothing left to feel. I guess these are my final moments—what else am I supposed to do other than accept my fate? It's a disappointing one, I have to admit. For all the trouble he caused, Rene sure didn't have anything interesting to say. His motives lacked intrigue or ingenuity. His plot is riddled with holes. How am I meant to cower in abhorrence at such a simple man? Simple. The plan was so simple it inevitably went belly up. Perhaps he would say the success lies in eliminating me, but my torture is only an afterthought. All people wish to go out in a glorious way—maybe I'm disappointed that my destruction is so mundane. A rivalry between two jazz clubs became my downfall. How trite.

I can't hear any noise from upstairs. I was never able to. This cellar must be compacted and sealed—though I don't wait in anticipation for my death, I am curious how long I've been sitting here, and how much time I have left. I never realized how much I would miss looking at a clock, watching the hands taunt me as time flew by and I did nothing to seize it. If I could make a dying wish, I'd ask to see the time. What a small thing we take for granted. I think it would put me at ease, right before Rene tears me apart with a knife.

Then I hear footsteps. Heels clacking on the steps outside the door, neither of which I can view. I strain my eyes and all that appears before me is oblivion. And then she emerges. Out of the shadows. Her cropped hair hugging her cheekbones. Her slender body tucked into a delicate, lavender dress. Telula. How can I be mad at that beautiful face? I hate this power she has over me. She's ruined me and yet I want to fall to my knees before her. These are the dames men write about when ships sail into port with no crew on board—all of the men were lured into the ocean by mermaids. But how could they resist? Anyone would fall victim to their tantalizing song.

I don't want to acknowledge her manifestation. I force my eyes to focus on my feet. They've grown just as numb as my fingers. I am radiating painful electricity. "Mo…" she sighs. I bite my lip. I have to stick to my convictions. They're all I have left.

"Oh, Mo," she repeats, rushing toward me with arms open. She collapses before me, throwing her hands around me. It's just an embrace, though. She doesn't try to set me free. Why would she? She grabs my jaw on either side and lifts my gaze—the pressure of her palms coerces me. We stare at each other. Perhaps we could have been lovers. The attraction between us is not just something I concocted in my head, hoped for in my dreams. She feels it too—she sends her wishes out to me. I wish she would have followed these instincts instead of her trek into cruelty.

"I'm sorry," she coos.

I shake my head. "No you're not," I reply sternly. I'm not begging to change her mind, to show her something she refuses to see. She's made her choices, and she's alright with them.

"I am. I really am." She pulls back a little. Drops her hands. She's in a crouch, ready to get back to her feet. Ready to walk away and leave me here to perish.

"Then why am I still here?" I ask. I shrug my shoulders—they barely move an inch. "Why am I still like this?"

"Because... because..." she stammers, "I need you to hear me out, first."

"You ruined my life. End of story. Nothing else to add I can't already guess."

"It's not like that," she insists, a perfect tear strolling down her cheek. She's playing me like a fiddle, right now. Weaponizing her helplessness to make me feel bad for her. To forgive her. She doesn't want me free, she just wants to be absolved.

"I'm not a priest, and this ain't confession."

"You don't understand—"

"Don't try that bullshit with me!" I'm furious. She really thought she could come here and sweet talk me. Her clean conscience is more important than my life. "You didn't have to do this. You accomplished *nothing*."

"But I did!" Now she's pacing, moving from feigned sorrow to unchecked mania. "Look, you may think 'cause I run with Rene that I have what he has. That couldn't be further from the truth... I've been working here for years and I ain't seen a dime. That man takes from me... and he puts my money away. Somewhere he says nobody can get to. That I gotta stash waiting for me when my contract is over. I *owe* him a debt he keeps changing the terms of."

She checks to see if I'm paying attention. What the expression on my mug relays. She sighs when I offer her nothing. "I came here for a better life. My momma tried her best with me, but she just couldn't provide. Single, working three jobs, I never saw her for more than an hour in a day. She hardly ever cooked for me, just left a loaf of bread on the table and told me to grab a slice whenever I got hungry. I didn't wanna keep living like that. Nobody would. I couldn't go to school, either. It took up too much of my time—I had to be out there earning to help her pick up the slack. I realized early on I didn't look like other girls... there was something special about me. I don't mean to brag—hell, my face has gotten me into more trouble than I could've imagined. But I was fifteen when men were offering me money to get up on stage and entertain a crowd. It could have been worse... I was in backwoods Louisiana, where manners still applied, so my songs were only vaguely provocative. But I got to sing. Really sing. And I loved it.

"My voice started taking me all over the state. People would scoop me up outside of bars and drive me miles away to the next city where I would perform for a new and vibrant crowd. I was making more money in a couple hours than I ever did bussing tables or mending clothes. I never told my momma that I left—I just took off one night with a strange man and never looked back. But I promised myself I would send her money. I just needed enough of it for the both of us.

"I wound up here eventually. Seventeen and naive, I thought New Orleans was holy ground. Boy was I wrong.... My first night I got into trouble. A club owner let me have my song but soon after pushed me off the stage and into the back room. He... he made me do things I can't bring myself to talk about. Gun to my head... laying on my back... men coming in and out.... Rene put a stop to it. He took a liking to me, y'know? He bought me off from the club owner and brought me to The Pup. But everything has a cost, and though he kept me outta prostitution, he made sure I never got mouthy. Or disrespectful. He kept me humble and in his servitude.

I should be grateful, though. I got a place to get some shuteye and a stage to stand on. When you came along, well, my money was threatened. If Rene was taking a hit, so was I. My poor momma... she's still out there scraping by. Everything that was meant to go to her is still tied up in Rene's business, and he assured me I would never get it so long as you was around."

"I'm not taking the blame for this, Telula," I say gently.

"I don't expect you to," she replies. "I just had to let you know... it wasn't personal, Mo. And I did my best to keep you alive. Those were my conditions."

"Come on... you see me. This is it. He's taking me out."

"I know... I know that now. I mean, I was just supposed to get a bit of extra sympathy from my customers. Maybe strike up all those deals that I lost with other clubs around town. New Orleans ain't the only place for jazz, though. You coulda gone anywhere. You still can. That's a deal worth taking, isn't it?"

"What deal? I wasn't offered anything."

"I gave you a chance to escape this place."

"Telula... stop kidding yourself," I say earnestly. I pity her, I do. That won't make me forgive her, though. I've been down on my luck, at the mercy of people much higher than me, and still I didn't stoop this low. I didn't delude myself to this degree. "If you wanted to help me, you would have told me what was about to go down. I was alone with you, wasn't I? You could've fake it—told me about the drugging and made me act like I'm asleep. *That* would've been a proper head start."

"So I'm not the best at planning. That doesn't make me a terrible person."

I'm not going to fight over her ethics. I'm not going to slander her morality. She's my ticket out of here—she's right about that much. If I can just convince her to untie my hands, I can walk out of here, once and for all. "You were trying to do what you thought was right. I get that. But I'm not the same as you, Telula."

"You are," she cries.

"No... no. Just 'cause you wanna say goodbye to New Orleans doesn't mean I feel the same. It's hard out here, I know. It's especially hard for us poor kids just tryna keep our brows down and work." She nods in agreement, more tears streaking her rosy cheeks. She attempts to collect herself; catch her breath. I'm wearing her down. "And you can still make this better, Telula. You can fix everything."

"I can?" She looks at me with her morose eyes. Her long, fluttery lashes. I wish it didn't have to be this way.

"Yeah."

She brings her head in close to mine. Her warm breath sprays against my neck. My lips. My limbs ache—I want to reach out to her. To close the distance. To kiss her, just once. Temptation is a curse. "Untie me, Telula," I whisper right in her ear.

She pauses. Considers. And then her arms are reaching around the barrel, working on the knots. She's got my hands loose. She moves to my feet while I toil over my torso. My veins are rushing blood to my expired muscles. My joints are slowly springing back to life. I'm free. I'm free. *I'm free.*

And just like that, I lunge at Telula. The smile on her pouty lips has yet to disappear, the shock not yet settled in as I gather the rope, force her onto her belly, and begin to bind her. "Mo?" she screeches, more in confusion than in pain. I'm silent, focused as I yank her fastened wrists and drag her to the barrel. "Stop it!"

Now she understands what's happening. I'm latching her to the barrel as she flails her legs wildly. "Help me!" she hollers at no one. They can't hear here. I doubt they even know she's down here with me. Her guilt led her here in secrecy, and now she will be found by Rene, an obvious traitor. "Mo, please!" she begs. I don't care.

It doesn't take much effort to corral her legs, and soon she's inextricable from the barrel. Immobile. I spit on the ground at her feet. "Don't you ever come looking for me," I warn.

"You bastard!" she yells. "I hope he kills you!"

Her true nature is revealed. She never gave a damn about me. Just wanted to save her own skin. Who knows if that story she wove had even a crumb of truth to it? That's not my problem, though. Not anymore. She can rot.

Entering the black hallway, I was long kept out of, I see the glint of light emanating from the door frame not far away. Funny, isn't it, to have the same experience twice? To begin my journey—my escape from the cops—with the same image I am presented with now at the end of the road? Life can be poetic, even as it's beating you blind. I don't hesitate like I have been—there is no pause for a deep breath, for an ear to detect movement on the other side. I am not going to cower anymore. Rene fumbled his maniacal plan multiple times—there is no cunning to fear.

I trudge up the stairs and emerge backstage. Wires and spare instruments line the walls. Curtains lay on the floor, patiently waiting for their turn to be hung. In the clutter, I spot something familiar. Sparkling. My trumpet—splayed on the ground like a piece of junk. I grab it, swaddle it in my arms like a newborn baby. It's the only thing that matters to me now—I fought to be able to play my music, to continue a career without interference. I love jazz more than I love myself. I will nurture my talent with the reverence it deserves, from here on out. My eyes dart across the hall, searching for the accompanying case. *Aha.* I pick it up, the smooth, black leather still intact. I nestle my trumpet inside. I'm ready to take on the world.

***

The Sun threatens to erase the night sky. Streaks of orange poke through gaps in the clouds. Nobody's followed me out of The Pup Café. Rene promised to return for me when his customers cleared out, and yet the building was silent when I left. Perhaps Rene was too afraid to face me again, to violate me while I was awake. While I was ready for it. Maybe he's afraid he won't hurt me, that his game will be nothing more than a pissing contest. I will die knowing he isn't even man enough to maim me. To live up to his word. Just like his clothes, he's incapable of reaching the heights he aspires to.

I don't regret leaving Telula there. I doubt Rene will murder her, especially now that I know how valuable she is to his club. She might get a scratch or two, rough her up to sell their story and let out some of his steam, but she'll live. Who knows, maybe she'll surprise herself and attack him back—she's had enough of his bullshit. Look at where it's gotten her? She's miserable, and desperate to leave him. Now, she's resorted to staging crimes with a despicable man all to maintain an elusive pile of money she's never seen and can't access. Why would that be worth protecting? He's probably lying to her. She probably knows it, too.

I previously resolved to keep the police out of this—I know I won't be believed, and I am sticking to my guns about that. The only smart part of their ploy was the irrefutable fact that all evidence pointed to me—no matter how compelling my arguments, no matter the lack of a dead body, I'm a black man with blood on my clothes. They could agree with my story and still throw me in the slammer. That's probably why Rene opted to end this himself—why allow the police into his establishment? I'm sure they'd find some kind of violation to charge him on, too, just for the hell of it. I'm not worried they'll arrest me, either. I'm not hanging around.

I guess Telula did get her wish after all, and in a sick way, perhaps this is for the best. New Orleans isn't the only place for me and my music. Surely, I'll be back here one day. When I'm untouchable. Dynamite. A legend of my own design. I pay no mind to whether or not Rene told his audience about me—whether he dropped my name and tarnished The Dog-House. They can spar among themselves, have a war for the people's affections. It won't include me. They aren't the only ears worth appealing to.

The early dregs of dawn feel like a new beginning. Is that a cliché? Yeah. I think I'm allowed some corny phrases and sentiments. I have had the worst three days of my life. I am owed some grace. I'm comforted by the coming day—something about the quiet streets, the gentle wind, and the aroma of bread baking in a storefront nearby, reminds me of home. If I do anything in my life, I hope it's making my family proud. I know they probably wish I'd come back to them, especially after this fiasco, but I still have work to do. Things to see. People to meet. They'll understand—especially when my name is on records their neighbors are buying at the store. I think I'll call them when I get where I'm going. They'll have payphones there, I'm sure of it. I could've been talking to them all this time, but I felt it made me a child. I had to solve problems on my own. But needing my parents isn't a bad thing. Their wisdom will guide me, make me a stronger man and a better person.

As if my parents were listening to me muse, an antique shop comes into view. Yellow lights are on behind the glossy windowpanes. Front and center, on display, is a beautiful, original radio. Cherry wood, gold decals, and that comically long antenna. I can feel the divots on the tuner on the pads of my fingers, the ridges now a part of my prints. The crackle of the static as the stations roll by plays in my ears. There's no sign on the door to tell me the establishment is closed. A clerk is at a desk within view of the front door. She's a little old lady, gray, stringy hair and overly large specs resting on her upturned nose. When I step inside, she doesn't flinch.

"Welcome," she says in an uncharacteristically raspy voice. It's almost masculine. She's probably a chain-smoker.

"Are you open, ma'am?"

"Of course. How else do you think you're in here?" She's reading the newspaper, a pen in hand as she circles words and details that catch her eye.

"It's just so early."

"Only six."

I chuckle. She must be the only morning person in all of New Orleans. "I have a question for you," I say, walking toward her immaculate table. The wood is so polished one might think it's been waxed. Much like all of the pieces of furniture and trinkets in the store, it's been maintained with a careful eye and a lot of love. The shelves and floor space around me are covered in items that have been dusted and posed for optimal viewing. I don't recognize most of these objects—perhaps I have lived too simple of a life to not even know the pleasures of a full home.

"Shoot," she replies.

"That radio in the window—"

"It's yours for five dollars."

I blush. "You see, the problem is, I don't have any money." I expect her to berate me, but she looks over the bridge of her nose, the newspaper now slack in her hand, and waits for me to explain myself. There is no animosity in her eyes. "I'm catching a bus out of New Orleans. I have one dollar to my name and I only picked it up off the street on the way here. That radio... it's something special to me. I have one just like it out there in the sticks. I will love it, I promise. Take care of it real good. Listen to it when I'm homesick. Listen to it when I'm not. I'm a plain man. I only need a few things to keep me occupied and happy."

She looks at the instrument case in my hand. "You a musician?"

"Yes ma'am. A trumpet player no less."

She scoots her chair out and comes out from behind the table. She brushes past me and toward the window. She plucks the radio off of its display and hands it to me. "I like musicians."

"Are you... are you sure, ma'am?" I don't know why I can't believe it. I don't know why I'm denying what I asked so kindly for.

"You pay me back by playing your song on that here radio," she says, retaking her position at her desk. "Only an honest man becomes an artist."

"Thank you," I say. "From the bottom of my heart."

"No more blubbering from you, boy. Go on and catch your bus." She waves me away and returns to her paper.

"Thank you," I say again. I retreat from her humble shop in disbelief.

***

The bus isn't crowded. I manage to score a row to myself, all the way in the back. The Sun has nearly risen, its half-moon shape slowly expanding. The cityscape fades into the morning air, the lights still off in most buildings. It's only a gray mass of low-rise buildings. I could have been the greatest musician to come out of New Orleans. I could have settled down there, ran the clubs, found aspiring artists off the street and mentored them. I could have changed that place for the better, but I guess dreams rarely come true for a reason. I don't need to be a savior. I don't need to be in history books. But, after all my failings, I still got a proper goodbye from New Orleans. My tired eyes ache. I lean my head back. Now it's just me, my trumpet, and my radio, ready to see what else is out there. Ready for a new night, a new club, a new jazz town.